BORDER COLLIES

Also by Iris Combe

COLLIES YESTERDAY AND TODAY

BORDER COLLIES

Iris Combe

═══════════

with a Foreword by
Her Grace The Duchess of Devonshire

faber and faber

First published in 1978
by Faber and Faber Limited
3 Queen Square London WC1N 3AU
Reprinted 1981, 1983 and 1986
Printed in Great Britain by
Redwood Burn Ltd Trowbridge Wiltshire
All rights reserved

British Library Cataloguing in Publication Data

Combe, Iris
  Border collies.
  1. Border collies
  I. Title
  636.7'3   SF429B64

  ISBN 0–571–14555–8

Contents

Illustrations

9

Illustrations

LINE DRAWINGS

Acknowledgements

My most grateful thanks to all those wonderful friends who have helped me with this book, and to the many people I have not met in person but who have supplied me with valuable information. A very special thank you to Her Grace the Duchess of Devonshire for her kind Foreword.

The information given to me by the International Sheep Dog Society and the Kennel Club has been of inestimable value. Messrs. Sotheby and Co. have been of great assistance in allowing me to hunt through their photographic files of old paintings of pastoral scenes and in giving me permission to reproduce some of these.

I would also like to express my appreciation to Dr Barnett and to my own veterinary surgeon who 'vetted' all the relevant information in Chapter 4, and a very sincere thank you to my friend Merie Byrnes for typing all the script.

Foreword

I am glad to have been given this chance to add a Foreword to *Border Collies*. After a beloved labrador died in an accident I did not feel inclined to have another dog and spent an unprecedented dogless six months. A friend said: 'Why don't you get a collie—you'll never regret it', and by a coincidence our shepherd's Border Collie had a litter of puppies at the farm at that time. I looked at them again and again in their shed and as they grew more attractive as they got older I had a favourite among them, and I asked the shepherd if they were all booked. They were—all except this one. So I was lucky enough to get him, and now I begin to understand the rare qualities these dogs have and their extraordinary intelligence coupled with the desire to please which gives them their special charm.

Their pleasure in working is wonderful to watch and makes one realize that they are surely happiest when doing what they have been bred for generations to do.

This book will tell us everything we want to know about this fascinating, useful and ancient breed of dog.

Deborah Devonshire

Introduction

Here is the story of a British shepherding dog, who by ancestry and working ability has proved to the world that he is second to none. The occupation of shepherding, the industry it has created and, indeed, a whole way of life, would not be possible without the Border Collies. Although shepherding in hill areas has changed little over the centuries, the occupation of the farmer has changed a great deal and the dogs' duties here are now of less importance, but collies have taken on many other roles, showing themselves to be enormously adaptable and versatile.

The evolution of this modern strain of shepherding dog is a highly complex story, full of much speculation and still open to dispute. It is not surprising that no one so far has embarked upon the full history or evolution of the breed from drover's dog, collie or farm dog, although many delightful and informative books have been written about them in their capacity as sheepdogs. After almost a lifetime spent studying and researching into the history and origins of collies and sheepdogs, I now feel I have sufficient evidence and experience to do some justice to the Border Collie's story. I have been considerably helped and inspired in my researches by accounts of the exploits of my great-uncle, James Bourchier, who was a correspondent for *The Times* in Bulgaria from 1890 to 1914. This remarkable man, who became a national hero through his work among the oppressed peasants and is the only European to have an issue of postage stamps in his honour, spent a great deal of time studying the herdsmen and their dogs in the Balkan and East Mediterranean countries.

It is quite obvious from his letters home that he found much evidence to substantiate a claim that many of our British pastoral breeds could trace their ancestry back to some of these dogs.

In my opinion, the Border Collie has not only achieved a very high peak in the quest for perfection, it has also now reached a new stage in its history, equal in importance to the one when it became accepted by shepherds and flockmasters as a sheepdog superior to all others within the British Isles. Since August 1976 it has become an officially recognized British breed on the canine map of the world. Although the Border Collie has long been regarded as a pure-bred shepherding dog, up till then he had no official recognition or Standard of breed points, except a brief one quoted in the *International Encyclopaedia of Dogs*. It was this startling discovery that led me to make a full study and investigation of such a curious situation. Along with many others I feel strongly that for the sake of future generations this dog needed a recognized written British Standard if it was to continue to be called a Border Collie and not just a sheepdog. Although he was already accepted as a pure-bred dog with an official Breed Standard in Australia, New Zealand and the United States, in the United Kingdom previous to 1976 he was officially registered with the International Sheep Dog Society and recognized only as a sheepdog; and as far as they are concerned in this matter they are, as their title suggests, acting solely in the interest of sheepdogs and shepherds and have never recognized the Border Collie except in that capacity. Almost every farm animal boasts a written breed description which distinguishes it from other varieties. It is important to realize that the fact that a breed has a Standard or pattern laid down to which it should conform does not necessarily mean that the breed need enter any show ring. Some people feel that by creating a Breed Standard or official description this dog will become a showbench variety and in time be subjected to the whims and fancies of exhibitors who may try to make the dog fit their own interpretation of the Breed Standard. Those who have opposed the idea of giving the Border Collie full canine recognition have acted from the highest motives, believing that this decision was in the best interests of the dog; they also believe that the only Standard required for him is his ability to work correctly, but it has been proved that in fact they were being over-protective to the breed. Then there are those few who feel that no one outside the farming or shepherding community should have any say in this matter, but these people fail to realize how selfishly they are acting. Not all collie owners are in the privileged position of having land and stock or the opportunity to work their dogs in this way, yet many may wish to have some other interest involving them with their chosen breed.

It is estimated that there are more of this type of herding dog in the British Isles today than any other breed, that is when one considers them collectively as farm dogs, those working in obedience and other tests, and as pets or companions. My claim is that this dog is unique in the canine world.

As this book is about the Border Collie in general, and not just about him in his capacity as a first-class sheepdog, it might be helpful here to explain the difference between a working sheepdog and a working collie. A *sheepdog* is any variety of dog that is trained to work with sheep in the manner required by the shepherd under differing climatic and environmental conditions. These dogs are usually rough, smooth or bearded collies, but I have seen other breeds working with great skill once they have been properly trained. A *collie* is a generally useful type of farm or herding dog capable of working with almost any type of stock and under most conditions. Herding is in collies' blood, as are other distinctive features. A *Border Collie* is the product of selective breeding from the best shepherding strains, but he is better known as a sheepdog because with the development of modern methods of other live-stock farming his work in this area is now limited. Further details regarding his evolution and title will follow. I often feel that if in the past this dog had been known simply as a British shepherding dog, there might have been less controversy. However, another British working breed and one that has had full recognition since dog shows began is the Cocker Spaniel. The owners of these dogs have always had the privilege of deciding whether to keep them as pets, working dogs, gundogs or show dogs, or a combination of all four categories, and the same situation can now arise for the owners of Border Collies. As with the spaniels, so too with the collies—there will always be different types bred for each purpose, and it is this freedom of choice that makes dog breeding, showing and working such an interesting pursuit or hobby—call it what you will. It could well be that the best-looking spaniel in the judge's opinion is also one of the best workers in the field.

It may surprise some people to learn that a competition was held, at the first sheepdog trials in 1873, for the best type of sheepdog. All the entries on the day were paraded before the judges, the winner being Tweed who was also overall winner of those trials. It was quite usual at that time to hold these 'type' competitions before the trials, and indeed even today these often take place either before or after trials, but they do not receive the same degree of publicity as the rest of the events. I have never been able to ascertain exactly what standard or type these judges are or were looking for, since nothing was laid down as a guide for them; one presumes they make their awards to the collie that catches their eye or is of the type they personally like best. It is true that if one owns a greyhound or a racehorse it is their performance on the track that counts, but they do also have an official description which distinguishes them from others of the canine or equine race. I will try to put before you just one of the reasons why I and others are happy that the Border Collie has how been given official recognition on the canine map.

Let us suppose someone from abroad, or even at home for that matter, purchased what he was led to believe was a Border Collie puppy and it grew up greatly resembling a Corgi instead. What would be his reaction? There is a Corgi Breed Standard by which he could point out how his puppy resembles that breed (or any other breed you care to mention) but there is nothing official by which he could compare its resemblance—or lack of resemblance —to a Border Collie. If he complains to the breeder or source from where he obtained the puppy, it is likely that he will be told 'its only standard is its ability to work'. By the time the puppy is ten to eleven months old it will definitely resemble some breed, but its ability to work cannot be tested until some time later. So if it resembled a Corgi instead of a Border Collie in shape it would be incapable of working in the manner which the purchaser expected from the breed he chose. I have deliberately quoted this instance as it did actually happen and was one of many similar cases where I was called upon by the authorities under the Trade Descriptions Act to give an opinion. When purchased at about nine weeks this pup, being a tricolour, apparently did in fact very much resemble a Border Collie puppy, but by the time the complaint was made, and when I saw this dog, it definitely resembled a Cardigan Corgi, with a lovely tail and short legs. Not having an official Breed Standard or description has given rise to many such cases lately, and far too many unscrupulous people are breeding or selling Border Collies whose only claim to this title is the fact that they are black and white. Now this situation has changed and the governing bodies who control the world of registered dogs have clarified the situation which was incomprehensible to all except those few who failed to see that it was necessary for this dog to comply to a pattern; yet he is built to a definite one and unless he is properly constructed he cannot perform his duties with the least possible effort as is required of a shepherding dog. The new official Breed Standard is quoted in the chapter on dog shows.

The Kennel Club is the governing body which gives official recognition to breeds when requested by a breed club or other governing body, so when the Border Collie Club of Great Britain was inaugurated in 1975 a request was sent to the Kennel Club for recognition of this British breed, together with a proposed Breed Standard; and the following extract is the result:

RECOGNITION OF THE BORDER COLLIE
(Extract from *Kennel Gazette*, June 1976)

The General Committee of the Kennel Club has decided that the Border Collie shall be recognized as a breed for show purposes in accordance with conditions set out below. This decision was reached after full and lengthy discussion with the International Sheep Dog Society, whose co-operation has been sought. For some time there have been requests from Border Collie enthusiasts that the breed be recognized for show purposes. The Kennel Club has hitherto withheld such recognition on the grounds that although there exists a recognized type, there was insufficient evidence of reliable true-to-type breeding. It is now evident that more attention has been given to developing the Border Collie as a true breed from the physical as distinct from the purely working point of view. The International Sheep Dog Society is interested only in the working ability of the Border Collie; it does not lay down a Standard for the breed nor does it wish to do so. It has its own registration system and its own sphere of activity (Sheepdog Trials) which will not be affected by Kennel Club recognition of the breed. Should any owners of K.C.-registered Border Collies wish their dogs to compete in I.S.D.S.-controlled activities, they will necessarily have to effect appropriate membership registrations with the I.S.D.S. Registration with the Kennel Club will not suffice. (It should be noted the International Sheep Dog Society will only accept a dog for registration if both parents are I.S.D.S. registered or if it is proved an outstanding working dog.)

It will be noted that this formal or official recognition in no way affects the breeding, training and selecting of these dogs for work of any description. Those people who have regarded that the Standard of these dogs should only be measured by their ability to work, will continue to do so, and will breed to their own type and Standard. This is still their privilege. However, recognition by the Kennel Club will give those other owners of Border Collies a new freedom of choice and, most important of all, it has established the Border Collie as a recognized breed and not just a herding dog.

There is a whole world of Border Collie owners outside the world of the farm dog, the hill dog, or the trials winner—and the pride of these owners in their dogs deserved some formal recognition. As I saw the situation, their enthusiasm was like a flooded river about to burst its banks which, if not guided into the right channels, could damage the breed as much as flood waters can damage crops. The formation of the Border Collie Club provided the dam necessary to control this. As always in cases of new ventures or ideas, there are fierce objections on various grounds, but in the main most objectors believe that where progress or restrictions are necessary they are quite in order so long as they do not interfere with the freedom of the individual.

Whatever the future holds for the breed we ought to be very grateful to all those people who have spent many hours both travelling and sitting around the conference tables of the International Sheep Dog Society and the Kennel Club headquarters, and indeed in many private homes, putting forward for discussion and consideration the views and opinions of all the interested parties. Whatever these views, all have felt they were acting to the best of their ability for the future of these dogs. One cannot hope to please everyone, but we must surely all agree that a good compromise has been reached to produce a situation where all owners of Border Collies now have freedom of choice.

There are many factors involved and many problems to sort out before a newly recognized or registered breed can appear in the show ring; not least of these is the appointment of judges with sufficient experience of the breed. Breeders carry great responsibilities at all times, but when a breed becomes eligible for the show bench, then even greater responsibilities lie on the shoulders of the first judges, the governing bodies and the exhibitors. This is not the full story of the controversy over the Border Collie becoming a recognized breed, only the bare facts of the case, and I do not propose to deal with the subject here in any greater detail as it is now a *fait accompli*, but these facts serve to illustrate some of the complexities surrounding this breed, and I felt it was important to mention them for the sake of future fanciers. It will now be appreciated how complex is the story of these pastoral or shepherd's dogs, and that it is quite impossible to put the various points of interest into separate watertight compartments. Without claiming to have succeeded in covering every aspect of the case, I have always been able to appreciate fully most of the points of view put forward by all sides, and I will reserve my own judgement on the wisdom or otherwise of the creation of this new status, based on my considerable personal experience of and research into this fascinating breed.

Chapter 1

BACKGROUND AND BREED POINTS

Before studying the shepherding dog in depth it is essential briefly to survey the background and development of the wool trade and the rôle which this dog has played in our economy, for it was in this context that the partnership between man and his dog became part of our heritage.

Sheep and Wool

When man first lived in caves, sheep and goats provided him with food and clothing, as well as many of his implements and ornaments. It was at this time that man first used a dog as a guard for both his flocks and family. The caves were usually situated on the hills and moors, since the valleys were but swamps and dense woodland, harbouring the wild beasts that attacked the flocks. From about the fifth century onwards Britons began to clear these woodlands and drain the swamps into rivers, and small farming settlements were built up. Centuries later, the waters in the valleys were harnessed as power to turn the machines of the mills for a growing textile industry, which had previously been carried on all over these islands in crofts and cottages, thus symbolizing man's conquest over his environment.

It can be truly said that sheep have played a major rôle in our history and economy from earliest times, and even constituted bargaining powers between kings and principalities; certain breeds were exported to Spain and a peak was reached in our export trade in 1273. In 1394, they formed a part of the marriage dowry of Catherine Plantagenet to Henry III of Spain, with far-reaching consequences in our history and economic development. Our top-grade fleeces were regularly exported to the Netherlands to be woven into the famous rugs and tapestries of that country. Political events on the continent were now claiming more attention from Parliament than the war against the Scots, so the battlefield was switched to Flanders.

Earlier, in 1336, King Edward III had decreed an embargo on these exports in the hope of saving money which he badly needed for this new campaign. Men at the back of this highly organized wool industry, fearing that this embargo would ruin their trade, formed themselves into a 'monopoly' and offered the King financial assistance in return for certain privileges. A new system for exporting was agreed upon between the King and the monopoly, called a 'staple'. It was agreed that the wool would be exported only through certain towns and ports where all taxes and revenue could be collected and shared between them and the King, to be known as a Staple Port. From this time onwards the wool industry flourished, and the skills of the Flemish weavers have left their mark on our history and architecture. In the House of Lords today can be found a relic reminding us of the importance of wool in our history—the Woolsack, upon which the Lord Chancellor is seated when the House meets.

Is it then too much to claim that it would have been almost impossible to supply the raw material for this industry without a shepherd's dog to gather, drive and tend the flocks? The words of the famous Ettrick shepherd, poet and writer James Hogg (1772–1835) are as true today as they were when he wrote that 'without him [the sheep dog] the mountainous land of England and Scotland would not be worth sixpence. It would require more hands to manage a flock of sheep and drive them to market than the profits of the whole were capable of maintaining.'

Sheep are credited with being stupid, straying creatures; in reality they are cunning and crafty, with a strong sense of territorial rights. Often when a new owner takes over a hill farm, he has to agree also to take over the existing flock of ewes which know the boundaries of the farm. Before the First World War there were thirty-seven different breeds of sheep listed in the British Isles, and once almost every county or shire had its own type of dog to manage them. Today approximately thirty breeds are listed, but some of these are regarded as rare breeds, and the modern Border Collie is capable of working with almost all of them.

Shepherds and others

It is often said that our British climate is the best in the world, but it's just our weather that is so awful! Farming in our climatic conditions has had a profound effect upon the activities of Britons and has produced sturdy characters as rugged as their surroundings. Any man who can make a profit, or even eke out a living, from sheep-farming on land which can be used for nothing else is indeed a clever business man. He needs an uncanny knowledge of his stock, the weather and the environment, plus a sense of good timing for selling, or, indeed, for any of the other tasks connected with farming. My farming friends also assure me he needs a tolerant, patient and understanding wife! Add to this the ability of a competent dog trainer and handler and you have the background necessary for a good livestock farmer. Those figures so loved by artists, of hunched-up little men with pleated smocks and battered hats, or those other Christ-like forms with a lamb under one arm and a crook on the other, are far from the true image of a modern shepherd or flockmaster. These men are more likely to wear well-cut tweed suits, to inspect their flocks from Land-Rovers and hold a university degree in agriculture. However advanced his methods or machines in general farming, when it comes to sheep-farming he cannot yet replace the dog. I have the highest regard for the men who train these dogs, a task which can only be undertaken by those who have the ability to make the dog fully understand what is required of him and then carry out these requirements under varying conditions.

The Dog Himself

It will now be fully appreciated that livestock, man and dog play, all three, an integral part in this story. Before I proceed to explore the theories on the ancestry or evolution of this modern breed it might first be interesting to try to establish the origin of the name 'collie' since 'sheepdog' is self-explanatory. I can only quote my own findings on this question, which may be open to dispute, but in the course of my investigations I was unable to find anyone who could provide me with any positive description or alternative authentic proof, although many other theories have been put forward.

The old Gaelic rural term for anything useful is 'collie' and for anything black is 'coly'. I refer here to the sort of Gaelic dialect as spoken among farming folk, not the true Gaelic language as found in textbooks. (I learned Gaelic in my youth at school.) So a collie dog was a useful farm dog, and in Scotland the names of many farm utensils are prefixed by the word 'collie'.

The Romans first classified canines into hunting dogs, guarding dogs, and shepherd's dogs, and used them all to full advantage. In 116 B.C. a Roman by the name of Marcus Terentius Varro was credited with having written hundreds of works on pastoral matters; his treatise on the care and training of the shepherd's dog makes wonderful reading and contains much information and advice which makes good sense even today. There is no doubt that these conquerors of our land made as much impact on the pastoral scene of these islands as they did on our cities, for they were very efficient farmers.

At one time the character of the shepherd's dog was a combination of all the above attributes or classifications. Therefore it is no wonder that over the centuries he became known as a collie dog, or useful farm dog. No more accurate description could be applied to the breed we know today as the Border Collie, for he is a dog capable of working with any kind of stock, under almost all climatic conditions; but careful selection over the centuries has bred out the hunting and attacking instincts and preserved the more gentle qualities. In examining the prefix word 'Border' my researching proved a little easier. James Reid, an Airdrie solicitor from sheep-farming background, and one-time Secretary of the International Sheep Dog Society, in fact gave the name 'Border Collie' to this new strain and inserted this title into the registration forms of the Society. In the latter years of the last century and the beginning of this one, the best specimens of working collies were to be found among the big sheep runs of the border counties between England and Scotland.

We may conclude then that a dog working solely with sheep is called a 'sheepdog' but that a 'collie dog' is one capable of working with any form of livestock. Further details regarding the correct title of these dogs crop up in the chapter on trials, so I will pass on to study the development or evolution of these shepherding or herding dogs, which I find necessary to divide into three separate stages.

EARLY DEVELOPMENT OF PASTORAL DOGS

This account is not so much connected with the history and origins of these dogs as with the development of a partnership between man and his dog, born of mutual trust and an appreciation of how each is dependent upon the other under various environmental conditions. I hope that this approach to the evolution of our present-day herding dogs will make interesting reading while at the same time giving the background to the characteristics found in present-day collies. I propose to cover several centuries in a few pages.

Mutual trust first had to be established between man and dog for both were hunters, and even today these instincts which are very much alive in all breeds of dog need to be controlled by upbringing and training. A modern collie who takes it into his head to go hunting is useless as a worker, but many kept as pets or for general farm work are excellent rabbiters. My husband has used two very successfully as gundogs and I will produce more evidence of this accomplishment later.

Once this mutual trust was achieved, the dog became more domesticated and trainable. He ceased to be a pack animal, soon discovering that his master's larder provided a quicker and more rewarding meal than he could find by hunting for it. Over a period of time his guarding instincts were exploited and the use of a dog made it possible to keep larger flocks or herds safe from attacks by wolves or other predators. The wolf was thought to be extinct in these islands by about A.D. 959 due largely to the efforts of Ludwell, Prince of Wales, and the pastoral dogs at that time were known as shepherd's hounds. Later, they acquired other skills and became true herding dogs.

We now move on to the fifteenth and sixteenth centuries when the rôle of the shepherd's dog was as essential as farm implements are today. In times of war farming is almost more important than in times of peace and over the centuries these islands have had their fair share of strife. Armies created a big demand for cattle, sheep and goats for victualling, and the hides and fleeces for clothing and equipment. Army rations moved with the camp, and usually on the hoof. Goats were especially important as they were comparatively easy to keep, feed and move, and every part of the animals served some useful purpose. The dogs that tended the herds became adept refuse collectors so it is no wonder that they have always been regarded as among the most ardent 'camp followers'.

Later on, in the heyday of droving, gangs of men worked as teams; indeed often entire families were involved and the dogs were trained for definite tasks on the drives. It could take months to move a large mixed flock or herd from one part of the country to another and armies could use up local stocks very quickly. There were few roads at that time, mainly those made by the Romans, and fencing was usually confined to natural barriers, which meant that teams of dogs were essential to keep the flocks together either when resting or moving. Pastures for feeding and watering caused few problems. Close to every inn was a paddock or small pound where animals could be rested, fed and watered, while the drovers also took refreshment. Many innkeepers earned a few pence on the side as dealers or informers. They could be relied upon to know of a supply of any commodity from a gallon of oil to a pony or brace of pheasants. Large rivers could only be crossed where bridges existed, which often meant long detours. It was at this period that the 'herding', 'driving' and 'holding' dog had his own separate task. A 'holding' dog was one capable of dragging down a sheep or even a cow and holding it in that position for examination or attention. Today any Border Collie can 'hold' sheep just by the use of their 'eye'. One further type was also used for hunting, to provide food for both men and dogs, later becoming known as a lurcher. These were crosses between shepherd's dogs and local breeds suited to local conditions and environments; thus a terrier was often one parent in Northern counties, and a greyhound in flatter expanses of country. Apart from sheer physical strength and stamina the requirements of a drover's dog are good herding ability, great courage, common sense or instinct, and a well-developed sense of self-preservation.

Centuries later, drover's dogs and many farm dogs were referred to as 'curs' by reason of having their tails cut off or 'curtailed'. The tail docking ceased but the name remained until the beginning of this century. At one time all dogs were liable to a tax, but a shepherd's dog was exempt if it had its tail docked, and should these dogs trespass en route or in the course of their normal duties as sheep or farm dogs, the distinctive mark of the docked tail would save them from the wrath of the gamekeeper, as it was believed that docking slowed down their agility when chasing or killing game. However, this tax failed in its purpose and was abolished, as it was found that many noblemen also had their hounds and sporting dogs docked, caring more for the saving on their purses than the general appearance of their dogs. A new tax on dogs was introduced in 1796 but it did not make this requirement. It was revised in 1878, and again the shepherd's dog became exempt. In 1959 another new tax on dogs was introduced, known as the Dog Licences Act, which was amended in 1969 and is still in force, although a dog doing *bona fide* work with sheep or cattle is exempt.

The rearing of livestock on the hills and in the valleys continued through times of war and peace. It was only when the animals were ready for their eventual destination that the drovers took over; sometimes, of course, a farmer or shepherd would personally carry out the full farming cycle from birth to slaughter, but he usually only attended the local markets as he could not be away from his herd too long. Sparse grazing on hills and dales is regarded as useful pasture for sheep and they are equipped to survive in this environment. The low-lying lands and marshes are more suited to grazing cattle. Writers and poets have always praised the wonderful dogs that gather the sheep from the hills, but a lesser-known though equally important part is played by pastoral dogs whose praises go unsung—the work of the dogs who drive the livestock to market. They were always referred to as collies since they were all of a certain strain, but in fact they bore little resemblance to the shepherd's collie; however, their work is part of this story. Cattle from the marshes that had to travel long distances were shod in a similar way to horses, the hooves being soft due to the type of pasture, otherwise, due to the rough roads, they might not have arrived at their destination in good condition. When geese were driven to markets or Goose Fairs, their feet were tarred and sanded to form protective 'shoes' while journeying on the flint roads. At a later date turkeys were also driven to markets in large flocks and wore little leather boots as protection—occasionally a 'turkey boot' will turn up in the attic of some farmhouse or in a rural antique shop. I have no definite proof that dogs were used to drive these turkey flocks although they might have been hard to control without them, but certainly the use of dogs for driving geese was standard practice in Norfolk and other parts of East Anglia. The cattle from the marshes were difficult to control, and larger and stronger dogs were required; the fact that they became slower in movement was due mainly to their having to drive this

30

larger type of stock. They were usually referred to as Smithfield dogs, or ban dogs, depending upon which part of the country they came from or on which routes they worked, since their eventual destination was often the Smithfield markets. (Originally the London market was known as Smooth Field as it consisted of rows of pens arranged in a square on a flat level field. In 1860 it was rebuilt and became Smithfield Meat Market.) These dogs were also trained to make a passage through the herds for the mail coaches or cart traffic using the roads into and through the towns. The hunting dog that accompanied the drive in East Anglia was said to be a greyhound type crossed with the drover's dog, and they became known as Norfolk Lurchers. They were a bigger type than those from northern counties, and later they became known as gypsies' dogs, due to their association with the nomadic life of the drovers.

The Smithfield dogs were woefully ill-treated, often being left behind at the markets to fend for themselves, so it was no wonder that they became treacherous and vicious and gave the shepherd's dog or collie a bad name among town folk. Indeed, even today among the older generation a collie is considered untrustworthy in temperament. It is a case of 'give a dog a bad name'. The drovers would have to work their way back to their usual market, farm or starting point, by taking seasonal jobs on farms or doing road repairs, wall-building and so on, and often they were unable to afford to take the dogs back with them. However, the hunting dog usually accompanied them for company and to provide dinners en route. If they were family men, the entourage moved too. Life under these conditions was simple; forest and grouse moors abounded to provide free grazing for the horses, goats and chickens that accompanied the caravans; fruit, vegetables and herbs supplemented the housekeeping; clothing and other necessities could be bought with money earned from the sale of rural craft work or puppies born on the outward journey. These families had priority of travel on definite routes and appeared each year or season at the same fairs or markets. The popular pastimes were music and story-telling, many a good meal or jug of ale being enjoyed at

31

town inns or wayside ale-houses in return for this form of entertainment, while the teams of dogs were left in charge of the flocks on the outward journey. On the road home any dogs or puppies that did return with the drovers were bargained for by local farmers. To a busy farmer who was short of a trained dog, one of these could be very useful at certain times of the year. Due to poor feeding and care, the fertility rate of farm dogs was not high, or they died at an early age due to distemper or sheer neglect.

I consider the drovers' dogs to be of great importance in the development of modern pastoral dogs. They far outnumbered the true collies used by shepherds or farmers who worked only on the hills and hirsels. The diversity of type has given rise to the differing descriptions of the shepherd's dog over the centuries. As has been seen, their treatment and care during this period left much to be desired. Dog books usually confine their contents to the more aristocratic members of the canine race and only brief references are made to the drover's dog. My information has been gleaned from old books and writings, parish histories concerning customs, folklore and the daily happenings of rural life in the past. Some of the laws and customs governing common land and forest grazing today go back to medieval times, and it is surprising how many of these concern dogs, rights and customs of tenants on hill or lowland farms; the shepherd's privilege to bring his dog to the kirk is just one of these. The story of these 'nomad-like' people is fascinating, though naturally we are only concerned with their dogs in this context. Over the centuries the more progressive of the drovers bought farms or parcels of land, others became hired herdsmen on the great estates. The skills and crafts connected with their way of life and knowledge of livestock and weather conditions were invaluable to their new masters. Those who lacked the desire or the opportunity to settle down to this new way of life remained as nomads, gypsies or tinkers as we know them today— not to be confused with the real continental Romany.

After this brief survey, it is time to pass on to observe the development of definite strains of collie during the prosperous era in British farming which followed.

ESTABLISHED TYPES OR STRAINS

From about the eighteenth century onwards rural and industrial life became increasingly interdependent, and one of the basic raw materials for the new industries that we are concerned with here was derived from sheep and cattle. Water power turned the wheels in the new mills, tanneries and workshops which were built along the valleys of the border counties close to the big sheep runs. In the early stages the raw material was delivered on the hoof to local slaughterhouses; the fleeces, the coal and other commodities then came by pack-horse to distant mills, and this method of transport makes fascinating history. Other development areas were East Anglia, the Cotswolds and part of South-east England where the invasion of continental weavers brought much prosperity and a high degree of culture.

Among the established types of pastoral dogs from the past whose blood most certainly must have intermingled with present-day Border Collies we must first consider the dogs from Wales. In James Bourchier's opinion both the goats and the dogs in Wales originally came from North Africa, and the now almost extinct herding dog known as the Welsh Hillman bore a great resemblance both physically and in method of working to a type of dog used by the goat-herds in those regions. In certain North African countries religious orders consider the dog an unclean animal because of its scavenging habits, but where they are used for herding a very pure strain is usually kept and well looked after, since the owners appreciate the worth of these dogs.

Another separate strain was known as the Welsh Grey which was particularly good at managing the large flocks of Feral goats which at one time outnumbered the sheep in the Principality. These goats are now almost wild creatures and are only found in some remote areas near Snowdonia, but there are a few herds in Scotland. The strong connection with goats in the Principality still remains alive today and two Welsh regiments—the Royal Welsh Fusiliers and Royal Welsh Regiment—have a goat as the regimental mascot. Other dogs from Wales like the Pembroke and Cardigan Corgis, though regarded as shepherding breeds, worked mainly with cattle, their size and method of working being especially useful for herding between the boats and the trains at the ports in the counties they are named after; but it is doubtful if their blood could have been intermingled with collies, more likely with local types of dogs called Heelers.

Next we should consider the Highland Collie, a different strain altogether, which remained comparatively pure in type until the Victorian era, when the interest of the Queen and her children gave him a new popularity and status. He was a well-built dog with a heavy coat and noble stature. He needed these qualities to deal with the wild mountain sheep, fierce highland cattle and the rugged terrain. It is supposed that a true Highland Collie has double dewclaws on his hind legs, to prevent him from sinking too deep into snow or mud. Historians tell us that these dogs are descended from the mountain dogs of the continent who all have this pecularity. I once owned one of these collies and he did in fact have these extra dewclaws. So much has been written about these dogs that I will dwell no further on them here, but I felt it appropriate to mention them since they too played their part in the evolution of the Border Collie. Pictures elsewhere in this book will help to show the difference between the Highland and Lowland Collies.

We read a great deal about the shepherding dogs of Scotland and the Border counties of Northern England, but at one time almost every county or shire had a separate strain of pastoral dog, each developed and used for a particular task. Devon and Cornwall seem to favour a large powerful type of dog, often looking like a cross between a Bearded Collie and an Old English Sheepdog. Shepherds in the counties of Sussex, Somerset, Wiltshire and bordering counties each had very definite types suited to their different breeds of sheep. One of the best known was the Dorset Sheepdog, a very fierce and faithful strain said to be the only type that could manage the headstrong Portland sheep. In Adelaide Gosset's book *Shepherds of Britain* written in 1900, a chapter concerning Dorset states that 'the grazing is generally flat, but the sheep are but roughly attended to; they are however folded at night. The English sheepdog is used, the Portland sheep are said to resent the collie and butt him.' Shepherds on the marshes have always tended to use a dog having the appearance of the Border Collie.

One of the most interesting aspects surrounding those old-type sheepdogs was the tremendous physical strength and the courage needed in the management of these flocks. Most of these breeds of sheep had huge horns, often two pairs, and those from the Isle of Man were particularly truculent. A famous strain of collies was worked by shepherds on the estates of the Dukes of Bedford, known as the 'Woburn pack'. The estates employed shepherds from the Highlands and Lowlands of Scotland who brought their dogs with them, and these dogs formed the foundation stock. It is known that some of the early show collies came from this stock and several are entered as winners at shows in the Kennel Club Stud Book under the titles of Lowland or Highland Collies, depending from where they originated.

Another famous strain, this time in the North country, known as 'Lordie's' or 'Laudie's pups' was used by shepherds and farmers on the estates of the Earls of Lonsdale. There are many good tales concerning these dogs. On these big estates shepherds and game-keepers worked very closely together with the same object in view; to produce better livestock and better dogs to work them. So it needs very little imagination to see how good dogs from each breed might have been cross-bred in order to produce even better dogs, or strengthen a special feature if possible.

I also found a reference by Ralph Fleesh, written in 1910, regarding sheepdogs of Ireland: 'In appearance the Irish sheepdog strongly resembles the old Scotch Border Collie—the 'bobtail', though seen in some parts, is not common.' However, pictures of all these dogs and of many from other counties in England show him to be the shape and size of a modern Border Collie with a Beardie type of coat, but he appeared to be black and white, which is unusual colouring for either a true Beardie or English Bobtail. It is interesting, too, that what has always been regarded as the true collie from the lowlands and border counties of Scotland (or North Britain as it was called then) was often included in old paintings of pastoral scenes. This would give further support to my theory that collies were used for general farm work, and the sheepdog for sheep only.

Apart from the invention of the plough, the one really important factor which revolutionized our agricultural and industrial life was the coming of the railway and steam engine. As this form of transport improved and extended all over Britain, it was no longer necessary for livestock to travel by road. Dogs transported, often unaccompanied, made it easier to obtain the services of a good dog from a well-known strain. It was in the North of England (and later in the West Country) that the railway system first began to be such an important form of transport; thus it was in the border counties of England and Scotland, where there was already a concentration of good dogs, that most progress was made in the evolution of the new strain of collie suitable for new methods of livestock farming. The railways even used collie dogs on some stretches of line to keep sheep and cows from wandering along the track. By this time all these varieties of collie, together with the droving dogs, had been selected into established strains and were more carefully bred from for their suitability for work with a particular breed of sheep or cattle. However, even at the turn of this century writers on farming matters referred to the dogs on English farms as sheepdogs, but collies when Scottish matters were being discussed. I have given fuller details of these dogs and other British shepherding dogs in my previous book on the subject (*Collies Yesterday and Today*, published in a limited edition in 1972), and I mention them here because doubtless somewhere in the past they must have intermingled with other collies or sheepdogs in the Principality.

EVOLUTION OF THE BORDER COLLIE

Good animals do not appear overnight; they evolve over a period of time, by process of the survival of the fittest and by careful breeding and selection. The Border Collie is just such a product and, as we have seen, he carries the blood of the early drovers' and shepherds' dogs in his veins; he also inherits all their instincts and qualities, so it is not surprising that as a worker he has superseded all other types of British shepherding dog.

Some authorities on pastoral dogs state that the Border Collie has been an established strain for centuries, but from discussions I have had with old shepherds or farmers, and from reading past literature in various farming or country journals, the dog we know today as the Border Collie is indeed a new modern strain, but descended from those collies of the lowlands and border counties of England and Scotland, mingled with the blood of those other strains of sheepdog I have previously mentioned. I want to make it clear at this stage that the rest of this book will really deal with our accepted modern strain, which is now regarded as a separate breed.

The coming of mechanization, specialization and new techniques in farming and livestock management meant that fewer men were needed for the various tasks, but large flocks managed by fewer men meant that more efficient dogs were thus also needed; and these were bred, selected, and trained by experienced flock-masters over a period, establishing many good lines of working dogs. Sheepdog trials also played a very important part as a means of ascertaining the full merit and worth of these dogs, and trials winners became valuable capital assets for stud and breeding, as indeed they do today. In the early part of the nineteenth century many breeds of dogs were rapidly gaining popularity, whereas up to this time they were regarded mainly as creatures for work, sport or the chase; in fact, the collie was so fashionable in Victorian days that he became almost a status symbol. The increasing interest in dog shows and sheepdog trials divided the breeders of collies into two main categories. The first was composed of those who wished to take advantage of this new vogue; they cultivated the trend for a beautiful animal, and good-looking dogs were quickly snapped up from farms. Later, with careful grooming and

37

feeding, they were exhibited. If they were award winners, they changed hands for big prices, but winners or not, once bred from and exhibited, their progeny could be counted upon as added income. The breeders in the second category were those who really cared for the dog's reputation as a worker. Some of the most outstanding trainers and dogs in the history of the Border Collie made their debut at this time. Then as today, sheepdog trials were the showground of these collies.

Many breeds of dogs were now becoming popular, but dog shows were still mainly confined to gundogs, terriers and shepherd dogs. The gundogs were owned or shown either by gamekeepers or by those interested in shooting. It was accepted that a gundog needed to be a good worker as well as a show specimen to be of any use, while on the other hand the exhibitors of collies were not so concerned with their working ability.

I mentioned previously that my husband has used collies very successfully as shooting dogs. A friend told me that when he was out ferreting rabbits his working collie would run ahead and 'point' at the burrows where the rabbits were at home. If she went straight past an earth or burrow it was no use setting nets as there was never anyone 'at home'. Gamekeepers, many of whom often combined this occupation with that of shepherd, believed that by crossing the collie and gundog, the intelligence and stamina of the collie might improve the working performance of the gundog, in particular the Irish Setter, who had always been regarded as difficult to train. Both the English Setter and the spaniels of that time were not unlike the old-type collies in appearance, as will be seen in a picture elsewhere in this book (Plate 6a). However, the gamekeepers never reckoned with the dominant genes in the collie, and most of the progeny of these crosses appeared to be more like beautiful collies than their original gundog parents.

Shepherds and gamekeepers are renowned for their reluctance to pass on their findings in the matter of breeding experiments, especially if these have been somewhat unorthodox or suspect. So one may assume that this inborn reluctance to communicate is one of the reasons for so little definite proof from collie quarters that these crosses did occur, and if so, whether the experiment was justified. One would presume not, at least from the sportsman's point of view, but the crossings did have an effect on the collies. It is thought that they are responsible for the particular method of working familiar to the modern Border Collie. It is my own belief that even earlier crossing or intermingling also took place between some of the droving types of collie and various gundogs, which was possibly responsible for the divergence of type, coat and conformation of future collies, as well as for influencing the working ability of both. This becomes an even greater possibility when one considers the conditions in which these dogs were kept—usually chained up or at best allowed to roam. A study of the photographs (Plates 5b and 6b) I have chosen to illustrate this theory may give cause for reflection on the subject.

By the middle of the century greater consideration was being given to the working collie and in particular the importance of his role in agriculture, and not just as a hill dog, was being much more appreciated. One presumes that any puppies bearing resemblance to the gundog parent would have been run on to assess their eventual capabilities resulting from the experiment. In copies of both *The Times* and *The Field* of that period there appeared many letters regarding sheepdog/gundog crossing and it is from this source that I have obtained much of my knowledge, as well as a great deal of information about sending dogs by train for stud purposes and to shows. Since many of these experiments in breeding for improvement were carried out by those interested in both gundogs and collies for exhibition, the resulting progeny was known as 'improved' strain, which later became the showbench variety of collie.

Personally I believe that these crossings had more effect in producing the show collie than in altering the working collie, but many believe them to have contributed towards strengthening the 'eye of control' and the pointing or creeping movement of the Border Collie; others disliked the spaniel or setter type of heads and ears that appeared in many collies from such matings.

With the interest of royalty and the growth in popularity of dog shows and sheepdog trials, both the 'improved' and 'unimproved' were commanding large prices for the breeders. Except in the matter of work, much more improvement was needed in the conditions and treatment of working dogs in general, particularly those on farms not in the public eye. There have always been men who knew the value of this wonderful new strain, who helped to build it from their own stock; but they were only a handful compared to all those careless owners who regarded the animal as little more than a slave.

The Countess of Bective was one of the first people to take some positive action in the matter. According to an account in the *Farrier's Encyclopedia* she maintained that 'this new strain of pure bred collie or one now considered pure bred by virtue of selection over the years was superior to those old crossbred strains and that his care and treatment was not in keeping with his new status'. She formed a Northern Counties Association for the Improvement of Sheepdogs and Working Trials, which encompassed the counties of Cumberland, Westmorland, Lancashire and Yorkshire; in fact the border counties where by the physical nature of the countryside the biggest sheep runs are found. This later became a Trials Society.

Many other sheepdog societies were formed about that time, but these concerned themselves mainly with the running of trials. In turn this helped to improve the lot of the sheepdog, since no one can hope to attain the high standard of performance needed for trials work with a half-starved or ill-treated dog which has received only adequate feeding and the bare minimum of shelter. Strict discipline and the survival of the fittest was the order of the day. This may seem harsh treatment to us nowadays, and indeed it was, but one must remember that rural life was a much harder existence then, and wages only bought the absolute necessities of life.

It is often said, and indeed I have seen it written many times, that the collies from Wales were always undersized from lack of proper care and feeding, but this situation was a direct result of agricultural conditions and wages. Today the working collies from Wales are among the finest specimens, but that part of the world

does seem to have a high proportion of 'puppy farms' and breeding establishments that sell Border Collies, or this is certainly the
conclusion one is led to when reading the advertisements in the
farming and canine journals. Perhaps this is why we hear so much
about owners having a Welsh Collie. It was certainly the main
reason for passing the Dog Breeders Act.

The biggest step forward in the story of this dog was the formation of the International Sheep Dog Society in 1906. Its aims were
to stimulate interest in the shepherd and his calling; to secure
better management of stock by improving the shepherd's dog; to
give financial assistance to members (and their widows) in case of
need. These objectives were promoted by the holding of trials and
the institution of a Stud Book for sheepdogs. There is no doubt
that the Society has indeed achieved all it set out to do. In 1915
James Reid, whom I mentioned earlier, became the new Secretary
and it was he who actually instituted the Stud Book, the first
volume being produced in 1955 with the assistance of T. Halsall.
The first entry in the Stud Book was a bitch named Old Maid (a
rather inappropriate name I feel!). We do not know why she was
chosen for this great honour, but other details regarding her
pedigree, etc. appear elsewhere, together with her picture. From
this time onwards this dog's rôle as a sheepdog eclipsed all his
other functions as a pastoral dog. Many present-day registered
Border Collies can trace their ancestry back to Old Maid and
Hemp, a dog bred by Adam Telfer from Morpeth in Northumberland in 1893, and sometimes called Old Hemp, the title 'old' being
given to a farm animal when one of its progeny is retained and
given the same name, usually because most breeders believe that
'like breeds like' and because it helped to identify the animal
with its sire or dam. Hemp must have been an outstanding worker
or produced good quality stock as he was the sire of over 200
puppies.

Having tried to establish how this strain of collie emerged, and
given details of his ancestors we will turn to the dog himself.

CLARIFICATION AND DESCRIPTION OF A BREED STANDARD

For many reasons I feel that this section may be the most important, yet the most controversial in this book, as each of us has a different mental picture of our own ideal collie. My real intention here is to consider in greater depth points from my introduction. In recent years it has become essential to draw up a Breed Standard or descriptive label for the Border Collie due to the new position of breeders and owners with regard to existing and proposed legislation in canine matters. Here is an example. If someone purchases a puppy or a dog at an agreed price and is supplied with the authentic pedigree and registration certificates purporting it to be a Border Collie, then the purchaser expects it to resemble this breed at least in appearance. If the purchaser agreed to buy just a good working collie or sheepdog and it fails in this respect, it could be the result of incorrect training or incompatibility. So, one may say, why not sell these dogs as mongrels or crossbreds? In this way, if they did not come up to expectations, the parties involved might avoid any legal actions; but on the other hand this would be a retrograde step and very unsatisfactory to everyone. In the days when one could purchase a good strain of working collie for about five shillings all this was of no importance; but today the offsprings of good strains can change hands at very high prices, and it is essential that both parties in the deal are fully protected.

I have always felt that the International Sheep Dog Society was the correct body to produce such a Standard, thereby justifying its exclusive rights in accepting registrations and issuing pedigrees for these dogs. On the other hand one must accept that according to its present constitution this Society is only concerned with sheepdogs, so at this point I will rest my own particular case, allowing the reader to be the judge and form his own mental pictures from my description of this breed. As a member of the Society and because I was also familiar with the requirements of the Kennel Club on these matters, I submitted for their consideration and, hopefully, approval a shortened version, without any explanations, of my following description before sending copies to other interested parties who were concerned with drawing up a form of Breed Standard that would be acceptable to the Kennel Club. Up to this time, these parties only had the Australian Standard on which to base their discussions, and later a proposed one from the Border Collie Club of Great Britain was produced which in my opinion was not at that time sufficiently clear. This is why I put forward my own proposed Standard, which will at least provide a basis for further thought and discussion when the present Kennel Club interim Standard comes up for ratification. Any attempts to preserve this purely British breed in its present state of perfection as a working or herding dog must surely be in the best interests of all concerned. However controversial all this may be it is indeed part of the very history of the breed and I can find no alternative but to record all the facts which the parties involved agree are correct. There will doubtless be readers with experience with these dogs who will disagree with part of what I have written; this is their privilege, and history has always been full of controversies. It is possible that in view of the new status of the breed the International Sheep Dog Society may now have to look very closely into its present policies on this matter.

Before embarking on a detailed study of this remarkable dog, it must first be understood that the modern Border Collie in no way resembles the present-day show bench variety of collie, rough- or smooth-coated (the former sometimes quite incorrectly called Lassie collies) except for the familiar white marking common to many shepherding breeds. A few of the early types did bear some resemblance to each other, since both were descended from the same ancestors, but more than a century of selective breeding has been responsible for the evolution of both varieties for totally different purposes. All good strains of working dogs are produced by serious breeders who study the performance and characteristics of the various types within the breed over a long period. When the selected parents are bred from, the resulting progeny are carefully selected or culled once again, and by this gradual process of rejection and selection a strain within the breed emerges with the ability and conformation which seems most suitable or acceptable for the task. This was certainly the case with the Border Collie and an acceptable and pure strain has been maintained for over a century. The dog upon which I have based my word picture is of the Hemp type since if he was considered to be of sufficiently outstanding merit to warrant being chosen as the sire for so many puppies then I feel he must have been the ideally correct type with which to breed. To make it easier to follow I have set out my points in similar format to the Kennel Club Standard, but all the wording is my own. All these points are the visible physical attributes which make up the character of any dog, but type, temperament and quality are hidden assets that cannot be written into any Breed Standard. The evaluation of them lies within each owner and they are often the deciding factors when choosing your puppy or dog. To me these features are the most important because if my dog's character is not compatible with my own we cannot be true companions. If he also possesses the required physical attributes of the breed then in my opinion I have the perfect Border Collie.

BREED POINTS OF A BORDER COLLIE

Characteristics

The Border Collie possesses a gay and inquiring disposition, has a great sense of humour, and readily accepts discipline. Once a bond of mutual trust and confidence has been built up between him and his master his devotion knows no bounds. His untiring energy can lead him into trouble if it is not channelled in the right direction. He needs to be bold and courageous—not timid or aggressive—apprehensive of strangers, tractable and obedient. He makes a happy and willing servant, but a rebellious slave.

General Appearance

The Border Collie should present the appearance of an active, well-balanced dog, capable of moving at great speed. Skill in performance is the paramount consideration. Adequate bone construction, a well-developed muscular system without coarseness, and great flexibility are essential to enable him to perform his task to best advantage with least effort. Great stamina is also required.

Head

The whole facial expression is one of inquisitiveness and alertness. A correct head pattern distinguishes the Border Collie from all other types of collies and gives the breed its identity. When viewed from the front it should appear broad and square in back skull, cheek bones not too prominent, the outline from the ears to the nose tapering only slightly to the nostrils, which should be wide open, giving a blunt end to the nose, which should be black. The muzzle should be well-rounded for good air passage, with plenty of gum space to accommodate the teeth and root system in the upper jaw. A moderately strong chin and underjaw are required for the same reason, making a snipey or weak foreface undesirable. Weakness here is associated with timidness or shyness. When viewed from the side, the skull should be flat, the foreface and back skull measuring approximately the same distance outwards from a well-pronounced 'stop', which is situated in a line between the eyes. The requirement of a flat as opposed to a domed skull is a built-in safety factor, and in the Kennel Club Standard mention is made of the occiput. This is often referred to as the 'bump of knowledge', but in fact I have usually found that dogs with a pronounced occiput are extraordinarily stupid. I like to see a fair amount of width between the ears and the skull reasonably flat at this point.

White Markings

The distinctive white muzzle and blaze on the head, together with the white markings to a greater or lesser degree around the neck, legs and tip of the tail, are characteristic of many shepherding breeds. The markings are thought to have been bred in by wise men of the past, partly as camouflage and partly to help the shep-

45

herd in poor visibility. Most farm animals have rather poor sight and it is believed that not only the 'eye of control' of the Border Collie but also the 'Now I see you, now I don't' aspect of the black and white markings have an effect on holding sheep. Most shepherds dislike an all-white or mostly white sheepdog as they feel that unless he is an exceptionally good worker he does not have the same power with the sheep or other livestock; so there may well be some truth in this camouflage theory. It is also believed that the movement of white feet or legs and the white tip to the tail often helped to guide a shepherd in the dark, as the light of his lamp could reflect on these moving parts. All the early show collies had these familiar white markings and I always feel that no self-respecting collie should be without them, but judges and exhibitors nowadays prefer the plain face. Let us hope that this preference is never extended to the Border Collie, but one cannot but note that these face markings have not been mentioned in the present Kennel Club Standard.

Eyes

Round, clear, bright, not too deep-set, with a forward vision. Mid-brown is preferred as too dark or too light an eye colour has a detrimental effect upon the stock and weakens the 'eye of control', as does the blue, partly blue or flecked colouring in the blue merles. Colour is very much a matter of personal preference. The 'eye' so often referred to regarding the Border Collie, is in fact the power of control any particular dog has upon the livestock he is working. One often hears mention of a dog with too strong or too weak an 'eye'. This 'eye of control' is an important feature and exclusive to the breed, the strength and quality of this ability cannot be accurately measured and must remain a matter of personal requirement on the part of each owner or handler. Many animals stalk and wear down their prey, but usually in order to kill. In the collie, man has exploited this instinct to good advantage. The infiltration of gundog blood and selective breeding has further developed it and established this unique feature in the Border Collie. In the matter of eyes, I simply agree to differ from the Kennel Club Standard, which requires that the eyes should be oval in shape, as I am afraid that if this particular shape is given too much consideration by judges, in time we may find breeders producing dogs with almond-shaped eyes like the present rough and smooth show collies, and this would of course be totally incorrect. In the show collie this almond shape is necessary because of the extra length of foreface.

Mouth

A full set of white, well-developed teeth, which should be set in strong jaws fitting together in a scissor bite. Badly discoloured

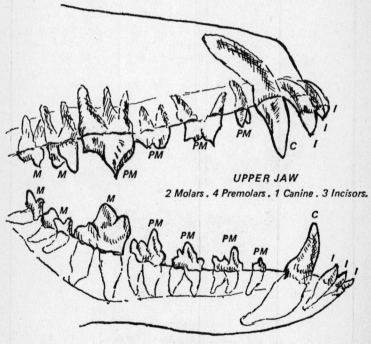

UPPER JAW
2 Molars . 4 Premolars . 1 Canine . 3 Incisors.

LOWER JAW
3 Molars . 4 Premolars . 1 Canine . 3 Incisors

Fig. 1a Upper and lower jaws

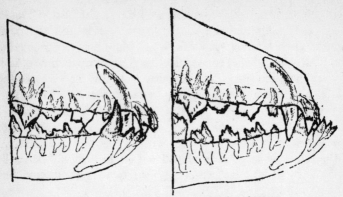

Fig. 1b Overshot and undershot jaws

It can be seen that in both cases of malformation the canine teeth penetrate the jaw, causing considerable pain or discomfort, and usually need to be filed down if the fault is permanent.

Fig. 1c Correct bite

teeth are often the result of an illness or the drugs used to cure one. Broken teeth or those carrying too much tartar should be pointed out to an exhibitor by a judge, as both are detrimental to the dog's health if not attended to. Show dogs are penalized for missing teeth, even if the Standard does not mention the fact that a full set is required. A requirement for exporting to most countries abroad is that the adult dog must have a full set and the correct bite. Undershot or overshot mouth in a fully-grown dog must be considered a fault. A full illustration of this point and the correct bite appears in Fig. 1. Malformation of the mouth will not, of course, affect the dog's ability to work, but depending on the extent it could affect his feeding, and in the case of a bitch it could prevent her from being a self-whelper. To continue to breed from stock with affected mouths could eventually lead to a permanent malformation in any particular strain.

Ears

Well set on the top of the head, giving an alert appearance. The whole ear is small, moderately wide at the base, tapering to the tips which may be bent over forward or held erect. There are two schools of thought on this point. For collies working on the high moors or places where they are exposed to driving rain and snow, and in long seeded grass or heather, the ear tips bent over give a good measure of protection. Dogs seen working on the trials grounds or on the lowland grazing tend to have pricked ears, the opinion being that this type trap the sound to better advantage and give a more alert appearance. The Kennel Club requires that the ears should be well furnished inside with hair, as does the Australian Standard although other conditions and requirements in the latter are very different. The purpose of this requirement escapes me.

Neck

A fair length is required to enable the dog to see his quarry in high grass, bracken or undergrowth, and the neck should be slightly arched to allow great flexibility of head and neck movement, without undue strain on the shoulder muscles when in the creeping or setting positions.

Forequarters

A well-laid shoulder is an essential requirement, being the basis

49

of all correct movement; a good slope of shoulder acts as a shock absorber. Forelegs should be straight with a moderate amount of bone, neither in nor out at the elbows. The muscular system should be well developed both over the shoulders and down the legs, with strong and very flexible pasterns, some feathering on the front legs, little or none on the hind legs below the hock joint. Excess feathering is a disadvantage to a dog working in snow as it tends to collect into snowballs. I do not fully understand the Kennel Club Standard on this point in particular with reference to bone (see K.C. Standard in the chapter on shows). All true collies have round bones (as opposed to the terrier types who have rather flatter bones) but the size and strength of the bone must be in proportion to the whole dog. In fact a correctly made collie has all anatomical parts in good balance and proportion with the exception of the upper and lower thigh bones. These are always slightly longer in a fast moving dog. The Border Collie, when working, keeps his hindquarters well tucked up and his forequarters well angulated, so for this reason when he is standing still and relaxed his back line appears to slope gently upwards from shoulders to stern.

Body
Back should be firm and strong, yet very supple; the top line should be neither dipped nor roached, having a slight slope upwards from withers to croup. The female, needing room to carry litters, may be slightly longer in body than the male; a tendency to cobbiness in either sex is undesirable. A very flexible spine is required for the duties this dog has to perform. A well-sprung rib cage is necessary for heart and lung movement at speed.

Hindquarters
The stifle joint should be sufficiently well bent to allow great freedom of action at speed. The hocks should be well let down and powerful, but not too short, and the tibia bone slightly longer than in other breeds. When viewed from behind, the legs should be in a straight line, standing moderately close together without

any tendency to cowhocks or bowhocks. Sickle hocks are not desirable. The male should have two apparently normal testicles fully descended onto the scrotum. Lack of entirety may not affect the working performance of a dog, but it can affect his ability to reproduce and is an hereditary fault. It is a very rare occurrence in our Border Collies, but every safeguard should be maintained to keep it that way; any affected dogs should not be used for breeding, even if capable.

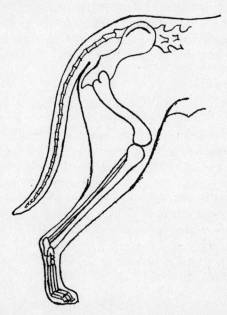

Fig. 2 The tibia bone in fast-moving dogs is slightly longer than in other types. The correctly set on tail reaches to the hocks. As over-angulation of either stifle or hock joint slows down movement, it will be noted that Border Collies tend to have straighter stifles than some other breeds.

Feet

Oval in shape, toes close together and well-arched, soles well-padded. The type of foot will depend to some extent on the terrain over which the dog will be working. Dogs working mainly over grass should have their nails attended to regularly. The removal of dew claws when whelps are three to four days old is recommended. In snowy conditions the hair between toes and pads should be trimmed to the level of the pads to prevent snowballing, and this also allows the foot to get a better grip on slippery or muddy grazing. Some farmers, who seldom ever look at their dogs' feet unless they are lame, may question this suggestion, but once they have tried it, they will be completely converted by the results. A horse needs to be well-shod to carry out his work efficiently, just as the farmer needs a good pair of boots, and it is equally important to pay attention to a collie's feet.

Movement or gait

At a slow pace and when viewed from the front the collie moves with front feet slightly turned in if the shoulder blades are placed correctly. Pintoeing or plaiting should be considered faults as these slow down and unbalance movement. Synchronization, perfect balance and co-ordination between forequarters and hindquarters are the keynotes to the apparently effortless ease with which this dog travels, turns and stops at speed. His true action can only be appreciated when he is working. His movement at speed is a study in grace when all his anatomical parts are working in perfect harmony. The crouching or creeping attitude adopted by the Border Collie is peculiar to the breed and no other dog works in quite the same fashion.

Tail

This constitutes the extra braking and balancing power of a collie moving and stopping at speed. It should be well set on, of fair length, reaching at least to the hock joint, well-feathered, carried low with a slight upward swirl at the tip, never carried above the horizontal or over the back except when the dog is young or at play. There is almost a whole language in the tail movement of a dog. Shepherds often remark that the brains are in the tail. Take note of the magnificent tails on most of the top winning working collies and you will appreciate the truth of this remark. A collie's special distinctions are his head and his tail. It is a great pity that in today's show collies few really good tails are seen. This has come about by breeders and judges paying too little attention to this end and too much to the other. Let us ensure that this does not happen in the case of the Border Collie. The reactions of a dog when he first meets a human or another dog are first indicated by his tail movement, and a study of this gives a true indication as to the character of the dog. A collie who carries his tail too high, or over the back, is usually a poor worker or may be too hysterical to train. If his tail is carried too low or under the body (except when he is frightened) he may prove either too timid for work or his temperament may be unreliable. In the wild state certain tail positions act as signals to other dogs. In severe weather conditions his tail will serve him well as a means of warmth as he can tuck his nose into his tail when sleeping, so that the breath drawn into the body is kept warm and helps to keep up body temperature.

Colour

Usually black and white, may also be black and tan, tricolour, brown or blue merle. As mentioned previously, an all-white dog is undesirable. The above colours may also carry the distinctive white markings of the collie to a greater or lesser degree. Colour in itself has no effect on the character of the dog or his fitness to work, but a collie with broken markings is known to have a less frightening effect upon livestock, especially sheep, than a dog of solid colour. This aspect was fully taken into account during the selection process while the breed was being established. Black is regarded as a colour that instils fear in a wild animal and was the original colour for guarding dogs. Interbreeding brought in the other colours. Centuries ago shepherds used dogs of different colours for certain tasks because of the effect of the colouring on the stock. Thus a black or mostly black dog would be used as a guard around the areas where the stock was gathered. Lighter coloured dogs like the blue merles or brindles would be used at lambing pens or where a quieter effect was required. An all-white dog would not generally be used, since under normal rural conditions it would be unlikely to remain pure white and therefore it would be difficult to distinguish it from the sheep at a distance. Today a white, or mostly white dog would only be considered suitable on its merit as a worker. The fox colouring (or sable as we know it today) as distinct from brown, is rarely seen in working collies, sheep having a great fear of the fox, but is sometimes seen in dogs working cattle. It is reasonable to suppose that the 'broken' colouring pattern of the modern collie is the most acceptable for shepherd and sheep, and, indeed, many shepherds prefer it. I note that the Kennel Club Standard is very guarded and diplomatic regarding colour, which will at present give great encouragement to exhibitors and assurance to pet owners and yet not restrict the judges. The subject of 'colour-inheritance' is fascinating, but it is too complex to be more than touched on here.

Coat
At present, according to the International Sheep Dog Society's registrations for sheepdogs, the coat texture may be rough, smooth or bearded. Here I will drop the word 'bearded' since we are now considering a Border Collie, the Bearded Collie having his own separate Breed Standard. I think the terms 'rough' and 'smooth' should be sufficient, as if the dog has a pronounced beard and shaggy coat and eyebrows then surely he is a Bearded type. In both the long and smooth variety the coat should be double. The undercoat should be soft and furry for warmth, with a trace of oiliness to make it completely waterproof. The outer coat should be of fair length, straight and harsh to allow water to drain off; a silky coat will hold water. The smooth variety, sometimes referred to as 'bare-skinned', also has a double coat, but the Kennel Club does not say if this coat is permissible in the show ring. The outer one is denser and carries slightly more oil to achieve the same weather-resistant effect. The double coat in a collie enables these dogs to work in most climatic conditions from extreme heat to extreme cold. Within a very short time the growth and denseness of the coat will adjust to the climate. The oiliness or grease in the coat is

often conditioned by general health and feeding, and it is an important fact although not visible to the naked eye. Lubricant might be
a better word, because when the coat is fully grown and the dog
kept groomed it gives the gloss on the overcoat and the weather-
resistant quality to the undercoat, being fed from glands just under
the skin. A thick weather-resistant coat is required, but an abund-
ance of coat would be a hindrance. A male collie 'moults', that is
sheds its coat, usually once a year, but the female sheds hers
approximately twelve weeks after she has been in season, which
may not necessarily be twice a year.

Size and Weight
Males measure from 18–22 inches (45.7–57 centimetres), females
from 16–20 in. (40.6–50.8 cm.) at the shoulder. These are only
approximate measurements to serve as guide lines. A collie either
too small or too tall would not be capable of carrying out the tasks
for which it was bred with the greatest efficiency. Similar remarks
may apply to weight, but as a guide-line a 22-in. (57-cm.) dog
should weigh approximately 45 lb. It is useful to know the weight
of your dog when certain medicines are required and for occasional
checks on his general health.

Faults
Viciousness, deafness or blindness (partial or whole), hip-dysplasia.
In the interest of the future of the breed it is recommended that
dogs or bitches known to have these faults are not bred from and
that all stock intended for breeding is tested for eye defects such
as Progressive Retinal Atrophy (P.R.A.) or Collie Eye Anomaly
(C.E.A.). Any departure from the foregoing breed points is to be
considered a fault if it interferes with the working ability of the
dog, and the seriousness of the fault to be in exact proportion to
its degree. This point is included in most Breed Standards and is
intended as guidance for those who have to evaluate dogs. In
effect it means that the virtues of the dogs according to their Breed
Standard are given first consideration. If a judge has in front of
him two dogs with equal virtues he will then consider the faults

and the seriousness of each fault. Suppose, for example, that dog No. 1 has a slightly overshot jaw, light eyes and a short tail, and that dog No. 2 has cow hocks, weak pasterns and is out at the elbows. In this instance the judge will place a higher award value on dog No. 1 because his faults will not affect his showing on the day or his ability to work. However, if a breeder studying his future breeding programme was evaluating these two dogs he would probably reverse the decisions as he would regard the seriousness of these faults differently. The faults in dog No. 1 are possibly hereditary and must be given full consideration in this case, whereas the faults in dog No. 2 could be the result of incorrect rearing or management.

Evaluating dogs according to their Breed Standard is a responsible task and should only be undertaken by those having a full knowledge of the breed and how it is constructed in order to carry out the work for which it is intended.

My comments regarding some points in the new Kennel Club Interim Standard are not intended to be deliberately critical. I simply want to bring important facts to light, so that they can be seriously considered at a future date when the Standard comes up for ratification. I feel sincerely that we should preserve the Border Collie as it is known and admired at present and not try to improve upon or alter it in any way, except by better care and attention. Much of the following information in this book is applicable to all dogs, but it is useful to have it all under one cover, and it is mainly intended for the help of the Border Collie owners.

REGISTRATIONS, LEGAL REQUIREMENTS AND PEDIGREES

International Sheep Dog Society Registrations

For a breed which until so recently had no official recognition the rules for entry into the Stud Book of the International Sheep Dog Society are stringent; so too are the fines for default. In this respect Border Collies are accepted for entry in their capacity as sheepdogs, but need not be used in that capacity. In order to register a dog one has first to be a member of the Society—subscription £5 per annum, with an enrolment fee of £3—and the registration fee for each puppy is £2 as from 1 November 1975. Many excellent working Border Collies are unregistered, as unless their owner wishes to work them in sheepdog trials, registration is unnecessary; but it should be remembered that progeny from unregistered dogs cannot be accepted either, and only puppies whose parents have passed the P.R.A. eye tests will now be accepted for registration, except at a much higher fee.

Notice of Mating

This is required to be forwarded to the Society on a special form within fourteen days of a mating having taken place and will only be accepted if sire and dam are previously registered. Puppies born of the recorded mating must be entered on a special form giving full details of their colour and markings, etc., before they are six months old. Fee £2 per pup. Penalties for applying to register them at a later date are very severe.

Transfers

Puppies can firstly be registered by the breeder directly in the name of the new owner, in which case a transfer of ownership certificate is not necessary, but if later they change ownership, this is then necessary and costs £1. For default on this count the penalty is £5.

Prefix or Affix

If a breeder wishes to register a prefix or affix the fee is £11. It is essential that you breed stock worthy of carrying your prefix or affix before you go to the trouble and expense of this form of registration. To start breeding sheepdogs today could mean quite a big outlay of capital. The price one would have to pay for a registered dog or bitch could be from £30 to £300 or more, depending on breeding and merit, plus the above-mentioned fees, but it will be money very well invested. In my own case, my prefix —'Tilehouse'—is registered with the Kennel Club and cost me £7 to compound for life, and I can add this prefix to any of my Border

Collies eligible for the Obedience Register. As I do not breed Border Collies suitable for high honours at sheepdog trials I have not as yet applied to have my prefix registered with the International Sheep Dog Society.

Registration of Border Collies Overseas

I.S.D.S. Rules for Registration of Border Collies Born Overseas

(a) The Breeder (the owner of the dam) must be a Member of the International Sheep Dog Society.

(b) A Service Card, or Notice of Mating (obtainable from the Society in advance) must be rendered to the Secretary within 14 days of the date of mating, and the post mark will be accepted as datal proof. The Society's administrative fee for acceptance of the service card is £3, or its foreign equivalent, and should be submitted with the card.

(c) On approval of the Service Card, the Secretary will send you an application Form for Registration of Litter, which should be completed fully, and returned to him within four calendar months of the date of birth of the litter. In this Application Form, you are required to give all relevant information about the Sire and Dam of the litter, their owners, and also a full description of the colouring type and size of each puppy to be registered, and of course, the name in which it is to be registered. Please remember that the Society only allow the use of one name (unless you wish to take advantage of the Society's prefix or suffix system), and the name given to the puppy must be appropriate to its sex. In the space allotted to each puppy in the folder, there are areas in which you are asked to affix photographs, three for each puppy, depicting Left Side, Right Side and Frontal View. These photographs should be taken when the pups are not less than three months of age, and they should preferably be coloured and not less than 9 × 6 cm. (polaroid shots are ideal for the purpose). The Registration Fees, which should be submitted with the Application Form, are £3 per puppy.

(d) A Certificate of Verification will be required in respect of each litter to be registered. The form will be sent to you at the same time as the Registration Form, and should be returned to the Secretary with it. Ideally, the form should be completed by your Veterinary Officer confirming that the litter for which Registration has been applied is the progeny of the Border Collie bitch named on the front page of the Registration Form.

(e) When Registration procedure is completed, the litter will be allocated numbers in a consecutive block irrespective of country of origin, but the Registered number will be preceded by an index letter, or letters to identify the country of origin. For example, B987654 would be a Belgian Border Collie, F987653 a French one, NL987652 one born in the Netherlands, US987651 would be a dog born in the United States and so on.

(f) Border Collies born outside the U.K. will be listed in a special section of the Society's Stud Book which is published each year and is sold to Members of the Society as a price equivalent to the cost of printing.

CONDITIONS FOR KENNEL CLUB REGISTRATION

(Extract from Kennel Club Gazette, June 1976)

Registration of Border Collies will be permitted only of dogs already themselves registered with the International Sheep Dog Society, or of dogs whose parents are registered either with the I.S.D.S. or the Kennel Club. (This procedure has always been followed for the acceptance of Border Collies in the Kennel Club Working Trials and Obedience Record.) The I.S.D.S. registration of ancestors must be quoted when applying for Kennel Club registration unless the parents are already Kennel Club registered. The I.S.D.S. has undertaken to provide relevant authentication if necessary. In the absence of such evidence, a Border Collie will not be accepted in the Kennel Club breed register. If one or both parents are not registered with the International Sheep Dog Society or the Kennel Club, the dog may only be entered in the Working Trials and Obedience Record. Applications for registration of Border Collies with the Kennel Club may be made from August 1, 1976. The yellow Kennel Club Form 1A should be used when applying for registration of dogs prior to August 1, 1976. The green Litter Recording Form 1 should be used for dogs born on or after August 1 if both parents are registered with the Kennel Club. However, it will not always occur that both parents are registered with the Kennel Club. In this event, for application to register Border Collies born on or after August 1, if one parent is registered with the Kennel Club and one with the I.S.D.S., the yellow Kennel Club Form 1A should be used for each dog to be registered, and the dog will be entered in the Basic Register. The same will apply if both parents are registered with the I.S.D.S. and not the Kennel Club. Border Collies at present registered in the Working Trials and Obedience Record will automatically be transferred to the Active Breed Register. It may be necessary in cases where an individual dog is already registered with the I.S.D.S. in one name to qualify the name in the Kennel Club Register by the addition of an affix or other word to avoid duplication or to comply in some other way with the Kennel Club Regulation for Registration. An even newer form of K.C. registration is now under consideration.

Kennel Club Stud Book Entry

Only dogs or bitches with the following qualifications are entitled to entry into the Kennel Club Stud Book, and must be the property of the registered owner at the time of qualification.

Show Dogs
Those winning Challenge Certificates, Reserve Challenge Certificates, or 1st, 2nd or 3rd prizes in Limit or Open classes where C.C.s are on offer.

Sporting and Gundogs
All winners of prizes, Reserve Awards of Honour, Diplomas of Merit at field trials held under Kennel Club field trial rules.

Obedience and Working Trials Dogs
Winners of prizes of qualifying certificates of Tracking Dog Stakes or Police Dog Stakes at Championship Working Trials held under Kennel Club rules. Winners of 1st, 2nd and 3rd prizes in Class C at Open and Championship Obedience classes or winners of Kennel Club Obedience Championship. Only dogs or bitches winning any of the above awards will be assigned a Stud Book number. N.B. rules and regulations are constantly having to be altered in the light of changing circumstances, so it is always safer to apply direct to the Kennel Club or I.S.D.S. for latest information in any given situation depending on the nature of the enquiry. The addresses of the two governing bodies are as follows:

International Sheep Dog Society, 64 St Loyes Street, Bedford MK40 1EZ.

The Kennel Club, 1 Clarges Street, Piccadilly, London W1Y 8AB.

Legal Requirements

Dog Licences Act 1969
A dog licence is necessary for every dog over the age of six months on your premises, but you can claim exemption as the Act states that 'if the dog is kept solely for the purpose of tending sheep or cattle on a farm or by a shepherd in the exercise of his calling or occupation it is exempt from tax'. Guide dogs for registered blind persons and packs of hounds are also exempt.

Dog Breeders Act 1973
This is another form of registration that requires anyone owning more than two bitches for the purpose of breeding to be registered with the local authorities at a cost of £2, but this cost may vary in some districts. The purpose of the Act is to prevent dogs and puppies from being kept in bad or overcrowded conditions; but

like many other Dog Acts it has failed to fulfil the purpose for which it was intended. Only responsible people who already keep their dogs in good condition usually apply to be registered and there is no lawful way of investigating premises such as puppy farms and back street pet traders. A person can keep any number of male dogs on the premises in the most appalling conditions and not come within this Act; but keep more than two bitches without applying for registration and you are in trouble with the law if a complaint is made. In the case of a dispute regarding this registration, the licensing authorities have got to prove that the extra number of bitches kept are for breeding purposes. Some may be too old, spayed or incapable of breeding for some other reason. It is a wise precaution to obtain a certificate from your vet to substantiate these reasons should it be necessary.

Trades Descriptions Act
The wording of this Act is too long to quote here, but a copy can be obtained from any local Council office or Town Hall. The sale of dogs or puppies comes within the terms of this Act. This is the important legislation that speeded up the necessity to compile a Breed Standard.

Import Restrictions
Under no circumstances or conditions can any canine and certain other forms of livestock be imported by any means into any part of the British Isles unless transported by the appointed authority direct from place of arrival to quarantine quarters. These restrictions now also cover oil rigs, boats or yachts in harbour, and floating hotels. Anyone wishing to bring a dog into any part of the British Isles either en route for another country or for a short or permanent stay should apply well in advance for accommodation in one of the Ministry-recommended quarantine kennels. If not, on arrival they may find no available kenneling.

Export Restrictions
Before exporting a dog or taking your own dog overseas with you,

it is necessary to apply to the representative office or Consulate of that country regarding the necessary application forms or other details, as in each country the laws differ and so do the types of inoculation or other health regulations required. Whether importing or exporting it is wise to apply for the latest information from the Ministry of Agriculture, Fisheries and Food, Government Building Block B, Hook Rise South, Tolworth, Surbiton, Surrey, stating your requirements exactly. It is also advisable to engage a firm who are experts in exporting animals to do the job rather than try to do the exporting yourself, and I have not found it any more costly. The anxieties and frustrations connected with exporting a dog are very real, as I have experienced, even with the help of a good and reliable exporter.

Pedigrees

To many people a pedigree is simply a piece of paper containing a lot of names and numbers; to others it is a veritable family picture album, but it is only when a breeder has been in a breed for a number of years that the names on a pedigree will become a picture and case history of each dog. I have often been shown pedigrees given to purchasers of a so-called Border Collie and when I politely tell the people they are not worth the paper they are written on they are horrified, and then go on to tell me how much they paid for the dog, where they got it and so on. Then it is my turn to be horrified at the ignorance and lack of care on the part of some purchasers. An official pedigree for these dogs is one that can be authenticated by the International Sheep Dog Society and one on which the names and registration numbers of several generations of ancestors appear. Without this information it is of little use. Pedigrees where dogs are registered with the Kennel Club need only have the K.C. registration numbers quoted for the dogs to which they apply. In both cases the registered name and number of the dog or pup must appear on the pedigree form and have the official stamp of registration. Export pedigrees can only be obtained from these governing bodies and not from the breeder.

There are, of course, a few breeders who can produce a pedigree which is absolutely authentic, even if not official, for each of their own dogs, but these are people whose business is breeding a good strain of sheepdog and the pedigree of each dog is more like a family tree. A very impressive pedigree does not necessarily mean that the individual dog it refers to is particularly impressive either for work or show, but by knowing its ancestors one can get some idea of its potential. Therefore it follows that a trumped-up pedigree with fictitious names on it is worthless. In some instances these names may be of actual dogs or bitches but if in turn they are the result of haphazard breeding or outcrossing it is still of no value.

All this legislation shows that we are now a long way from the days when, in the main, only forest laws or the rights of common land grazing were all that applied to the owners of these dogs, and when a pedigree dog on a farm was considered as useless as a pedigree gundog. It will be noted that all the above information applies only to the United Kingdom; overseas readers will be aware of any legal requirement regarding these dogs in their own country.

Chapter 2

BASIC TRAINING AND WORKING CAPACITIES

THE FIRST STEPS

It is not my intention here to elaborate on methods for training your collie, as that would not be possible within the scope of this book. There are some excellent books written by specialists on training collies and other dogs, to which the reader may refer. What I hope to do is to pass on some hints and open your eyes to the many and varied tasks that a collie can be trained to perform. First, one must establish what type of work the dog will be required to do. After this a partnership must be created between you and the particular dog that you have selected as being suitable for your purpose. Third, remember that each exercise in any form of training is based on the natural behaviour pattern or bodily movement of the dog. It is natural for a dog to move at all the paces we require of him, and for him to sit or stand; so there is nothing unnatural or cruel in training a dog. In fact, every dog—even a household pet—needs some training. A trained dog is a happy one, as then he learns the difference between right and wrong—a distinction that does not come automatically to him. If you scold a dog for doing something that is wrong in your opinion, he does not understand unless he has been taught that it is in fact wrong to do it. Always be consistent in your training and always use the same words or commands for the same exercise. Do not allow, or even encourage, your dog to dig a huge hole in the garden one day, and the next time scold him for doing the same thing. You will have confused him. Training is a fascinating business, for with each category one enters a whole new world of experiences and often one has to learn an entirely new language, to say nothing of having to understand local terms for certain situations, particularly in farming circles.

A bitch instinctively teaches her pups to fear man, so training begins in the nest. Most bitches with litters are apprehensive of strangers, even aggressive at times if they approach the nest; others are very trusting and will allow anyone to handle the pups. It is the first introduction between the human and the pup that makes or mars any future relationship. From the time the pups can first see and hear, the more human contact they have the better; this is where children can be of so much help. All young things seem to have a certain sympathy and understanding for each other. Pups reared in outside kennels on farms where they have little contact with humans are often shy and nervous at first, whereas those reared in the house or nearby who have continual contact with the family usually learn to take various situations in their stride at an early age.

The first human sound the pup hears is usually the voice of the breeder when he or she comes to feed the bitch or let her out. This will give a sense of pleasure to the bitch which she in turn will pass on to the pups who will feel reassured that this new experience is pleasant; at once the correct and lasting contact is established. This careful introduction has to be kept up continually until the puppies have learnt to take strange noises and voices for granted. The bitch herself helps here as the sound of your footsteps approaching or just of the latch being lifted causes her to wag her tail and come out of her box to greet you. This gives a sense of reassurance which the pups learn to associate with your appearance, and which is intensified by the sound of putting down the food dish with the resulting pleasure.

After sound comes smell or scent, the greatest single factor governing the reactions of all dogs, but as yet very little understood by humans. To the dog or puppies the secnt that accompanies sound also inspires confidence; the pups will accept human handling without fear once this has been established.

66

The building-up of canine and human relationships is usually taken for granted and will appear to be an automatic process if a litter is reared under normal conditions, but quite often litters have little or no contact with humans until they are five or six weeks old, except for one human who visits the bitch and her litter to let her out for exercise or to put down a bowl of food. It is very noticeable how long it takes for pups from these litters to come to hand and for any bond of trust between them and a human to be formed. This is why upbringing and environment often play a vital part in forming the character and temperament of a dog. I am quite sure that if many more handlers realized the importance of the part this first contact in the nest plays in establishing a real trust between man and dog, they would pay more attention to it. Very often it is the wife who brings up the litters, so she will probably talk to the pups and fondle them from an early age. This is where the 'getting to know each other' process will be almost automatic. Many farmers or flockmasters think it 'cissy' to talk to or fondle young animals, but a true shepherd knows the full value of this contact.

The next step in training is to get the pup accustomed to its name and to come to you when called, and this also begins with an association of ideas. Call 'Lass', then 'Lass come' and put down her dinner, and you will have made a good start. Never call a young pup to you unless you really mean it to come, and when it does always praise it; just a quiet word or a pat is sufficient. All of this can be achieved before the pup has even been fully weaned, except that you will find very soon that every pup in the litter will think its name is 'Lass'.

I have proved many times that this conditioning and establishing of mutual trust really pays dividends and halves training efforts later on. I have bought pups from farms where they were born in an old chicken coop with the bitch still on the chain, never having had any solid food, existing only on the bitch's milk. The farmer believed in the survival of the fittest and indeed this theory paid off in this respect; but it took me almost a year to gain the confidence of these pups and they never did get accustomed to strangers or strange places. On another occasion I bought a pup from a farm in one of the remotest parts of Wales. Again it was from the 'survival of the fittest' brigade, but she and the bitch had always had complete freedom of the farm and all the farmhands talked to and played with them. By the time I got her at eight weeks she was already trained to accept any given situation or human contact. She was a poor specimen through lack of breeding and rearing, but one of my best workers for stock that I have ever had the privilege to train, and she proved her worth later in the obedience ring. Everything seemed to come naturally to her and I always put this down to her early contact with the people in the farmyard. In due course I bred her to a very good working dog with highly satisfactory results.

Any form of training takes time and the most important part is the ground work. All trainers have their own particular areas where they excel, but very few excel in all areas of training. I specialize in the field of early training and acclimatization that is so necessary for a dog who has to cope with all the stresses and strains of modern living as well as his work. Only those dogs familiar with and accepting these stresses are of any use in trials or on the show ground when they have to encounter so many hazards, of which travelling is only one, before they even get to the starting post.

Once the relationship of confidence between dog and master has been formed it is time to commence the specialist training which may be for any type of farm work or for the obedience ring, but the basic principles of training are the same for whichever purpose. The first prerequisite in any form of dog training is that the trainer should know more than the dog; this may sound obvious, but when one is dealing with collies, trainers often overlook the fact that these dogs are so intelligent and so much one-man dogs that they have made a pretty detailed study of you, your habits and reactions long before you have observed theirs. You are now the pack leader to whom your dog owes his allegiance. You must both be working on the same wavelength, capable of transmitting to him clear and concise signals which he can see some point in obeying.

FARM WORK

In my opinion young dogs should never be introduced to stock unless they are on a lead as once they get the wrong idea into their heads, weeks of training are lost. For general farm work the rest of the dog's training is usually a matter of following a daily routine. On the whole collies are a fairly silent breed, but as puppies they are very exuberant and often rush about barking as they play. This barking habit must be curbed without spoiling the dog's natural gaiety. Collie puppies are also inclined to be adventurous, curious and destructive if left too much to their own devices. These happy puppyhood qualities are admirable in many other breeds, but in a collie intended for serious work they have to be restricted or channelled into the right direction without breaking the dog's spirit. In fact they have to learn to take discipline, while still wagging their tails and winking at you as they often do.

People frequently ask: 'are young dogs trained by being worked alongside an experienced dog?'. The answer is usually 'no', because they are more likely to pick up any bad habits and not the good ones. It is not possible to train any dog for work with a book in one hand and a lead in the other. I suggest that if you want to learn to train a collie or sheepdog you find an experienced trainer willing to teach you, and I should like to add a comment here on these forms of training. I have trained a number of collies for several different purposes including working with stock, but my methods in the latter case are purely those I learned on the farm as a child. They get results and are highly original if nothing else. Mostly the directions have to be given by hand signals as I have learnt to whistle only recently. Present-day farming methods, efficient as they are, have robbed us of some of the novelty of training farm collies and therefore much of the fun has also gone. We rarely use our farm collies to round up poultry, to quote just one instance, nor for bringing cows in at milking time. Most farm collies today are used for the management of store cattle and sheep.

The days of the small farm are no longer with us, when the farmer and his dog, having finished the early work with the stock in the yard would set off after breakfast for a few hours ploughing or sowing in the fields. The dog would walk every furrow beside his master and the horse—even sharing his lunch, and occasionally departing to follow a thrilling scent; at the end of the day he helped to bring in the cattle again for milking or shut up the poultry. This work was carried out not so much by any method of training as by following a definite routine each day until it became a way of life. Before the days of broiler houses and deep litter we fattened poultry for Christmas or other festive occasions, and after the harvest we used to put these poultry out on the stubble for free pickings of corn. Small huts like old-fashioned bathing machines were pushed out into the fields for night-time shelter and as protection from foxes. We had one collie who was wonderfully patient at this job, but as soon as the last bird was in the last hut at dusk, he would take a good nip at it, removing several tail feathers—he would then turn and really grin at you.

Training for work of this nature can only begin when the dog is already disciplined and has some basic understanding of your calls. All work here must be carried out on a long lead at first. He must never be allowed to break or chase for the fun of it. Your own actions must be positive and quiet. I have yet to find a collie I can get to come to hand for serious training much under the age of eighteen months. However, up to this stage, both the dog and myself have built up a pretty good understanding of each other, observing each other's pecularities and learning to anticipate each other's next move in a given situation. As this 'getting to know you' process starts in the nest, if you have bred the dog you are about to train then you have a decided advantage. Choosing the right dog for the type of work required needs experience and a certain amount of luck; indeed the latter is needed at all stages. If a collie is required for working with sheep the degree of 'the eye of control' will sometimes determine the choice; but each owner will have his own special preference in this matter. While also using his 'eye' the collie's use of body movement is important particularly when holding or moving cattle. (I have given more details of this unique feature of the 'eye' of a Border Collie in chapter 1.) The clapping or creeping action is rarely taught as it usually comes naturally to present-day Border Collies; in fact sometimes a trainer has to correct over-zealousness in this respect. If you stood in front of a herd of cattle or a flock of sheep coming towards you, you would only have the effect of scattering them and you would get trampled upon into the bargain, but a trained collie can turn them in either direction just by the control of his movements or the power of his 'eye'.

Basic obedience or discipline exercises are the first steps in any form of training. These are simple, such as 'come' when called, stay in one spot for as long as is required, walk close to the handler, or in front or behind according to requirements—a few minutes with each exercise is all that is required at first and should be done on a lead, as one has more control over the dog this way. If a dog is once allowed to get away with not obeying a command, it is difficult to correct him unless he is on a lead. When he is steady at the basic exercises on a lead, only then should he be encouraged to perform them off the lead, and when this point has been successfully reached then more advanced training can begin.

SHEEPWORK

It is as a sheepdog that the Border Collie excels, and I felt that my best way of describing the training necessary for this activity would be to base my account on the methods of a number of experienced shepherds or handlers. The latter were by no means always forthcoming, and from the time I first embarked upon this quest for training techniques it has taken me over three years to receive the replies and sift through the information. I am now beginning to understand in full the disbelief of some men that I should even attempt to embark on such a vast and varied subject. I will give you a summary of the contents of these letters which made me very much aware of the different methods employed when dealing with different breeds of sheep and types of farm. All animal husbandry is a skilled occupation, but with sheep, knowledge of the effect of the elements and the quality of the grazing at different altitudes and seasons is also essential.

The first pattern that became apparent was the age-old custom of a farming skill or tradition passing in a family from father to son. This must indeed be a most rewarding experience for both. The father will feel that his accumulated knowledge has not been wasted and the son will benefit from having worked side by side with an experienced man. Farming traditions and local folklore play a very large part in family relationships of this nature, and even the partnership methods of training the dog can be carefully guarded secrets, but the type of dog bred, and its training, will bear a distinct relationship to the type of stock or breed of sheep it is required to work.

The next clear pattern to emerge from the responses of these experienced people to my inquiries was the great variation in the types of sheep farms, depending on the part of the country. Hill farming is usually the most arduous type, and here man and dog need each other most. It became clear to me that in these conditions a strong, free-moving dog was required rather than one with a strong 'eye'. The Bearded Collie is a very useful dog for hill herding, his method of working being different from the Border Collie. He is adept at hunting out sheep from inaccessible places and will readily drive them along. He also 'speaks' when he is on the trail of his quarry, rather like a hound. For lowland farming or in places where sheep are folded and moved each day, a very different type of dog is required and the method of training is also different. Yet the dogs, both by their appearance and their breeding backgrounds, are all modern Border Collies capable of tackling any type of work. Is any breed more versatile? All the replies to my letters stressed the need to understand the requirements of the stock to be controlled before attempting to train the dog for that particular task.

I found that the most difficult aspect to grasp was how the trainer or handler, whichever you like to call him, was able to work out a separate code of whistles for each dog he was training and to remember each one, as no two dogs will work to the same set of whistles or commands. The whistle, either natural or manmade, is used more often than the voice for giving commands, as it eliminates any human emotions like anger or frustration which may come out in the tone of the voice, thereby upsetting the performance of the dog, and of course the sound travels over a greater distance.

Finally, all the letters stressed the fact that little could be learned from books on the matter of training sheepdogs—knowledge had to come from actual experience. Naturally I agree with this observation, but the opportunities for gaining such experience are limited, in fact so far as I can gather there are just three main paths of entry. Firstly, to be lucky enough to be the son or near-relation of a shepherd or farmer; secondly, to become a trainee shepherd; or thirdly, to attend an Agricultural College. Whichever path an intending sheep farmer should choose he is assured of an interesting and rewarding occupation and one in which, for the foreseeable future, both he and his dog are unlikely to become redundant, except through inefficiency.

There are good and bad masters; some could never train a dog, however clever or willing. I have seen collies working sheep with one front leg secured through its collar in order to slow him down or steady him. This to me is sheer cruelty and a definite indication that the handler is quite incapable of training that dog, or that he should have sufficient understanding to change to another dog since he and that particular one are not suited to each other's requirements.

While in Australia and some European countries I have had brief opportunities of studying shepherding methods and the training of these dogs. The basic principles of discipline and obedience are similar to our own, but the dogs tend to be used more in packs, with less opportunity for individual development of brain and character. Or alternatively in Australia and New Zealand some are trained for one specific task only in the herds and flocks. Shepherding methods are very different in these countries from those in the UK because of the nature of the terrain and the enormous numbers of animals involved (Plate 2b).

SHEEPDOG TRIALS

The training of a collie as a sheepdog is seen to full advantage by the public on the trials field. It is here that all the previous ground-work or breeding, caring and handling can be tested. I myself am a dedicated spectator. Training dogs for work in sheepdog trials is a specialized skill limited to some degree by opportunity and which again is usually passed on from father to son, whether he be the owner of the land or a hired shepherd. One frequently hears the boast that dogs run at trials are just ordinary dogs that do an ordinary day's work at other times, and this is of course true up to a point. But neither the dog nor the handlers can be said to be ordinary. The skill, concentration and experience of the latter are of the quality of an Olympic coach. The obstacles on a course and the general layout are made to resemble as closely as possible anything that might be encountered by the dogs working in or around lowland farms or hirsels, but the element of the special skills needed for hill work is naturally impossible to stage. Never attempt advanced training with a dog that you know is not the right material, for the efforts will only end up by frustrating the handler and probably souring the dog. As Border Collies perform all movements from the brain to the tip of the tail and toes 'at the double', unless the handler is capable of anticipating the reactions of the dog to his commands, with equal or greater speed, success in trials work is doomed. The material and the will to work must already be in the dog before advanced training can be under-taken. A good practical knowledge of the habits and movements of various breeds of sheep can often tip the scales between success or failure on the field.

OBEDIENCE WORK

Before I became interested in obedience work I trained a team of three collies to give demonstrations at local fêtes by driving and penning five ducks in a small area. The team consisted of a smooth show-type collie, a Border Collie and my champion rough-coated show collie. All were males and deadly enemies at home, but they worked and behaved perfectly when on parade. Several friends helped me with the props and so on, and we had great fun until the team was disbanded on the death of the smooth dog, following an attack of distemper and hardpad. When I joined a training club and later took an instructor's course, I marvelled at how I had dared to put on such a demonstration, but it always seemed to go down well.

The advantages from the human point of view of venturing into the obedience world are educational, social and in some cases therapeutic. The reasons for the enthusiasm which this type of work with dogs generates are psychological. There is a great desire in most of us to be master of something in life, be it the arts, academic studies, business, or just being a successful parent. As I see it, when the desire concerns animals we fall into two categories; those who wish to succeed or master the art of training by imposing their own will and methods on the animal, and those who train by co-operation, making a study of the individual character of the animal and adapting their methods accordingly. While the former type may make excellent trainers and instructors with many breeds of dogs, only the latter type will succeed where collies are concerned.

One can derive great pleasure from belonging to a local dog club and taking part in obedience training, but one must realize that the aim is not to teach the dog but to teach the owner how best to train his dog. This training cannot be learned from a book; it is necessary to attend classes and then to practise the exercises at home, although reading about the basic principles involved can help to a certain extent. Even if you find that neither you nor your collie are capable of reaching the high standard required in this form of competition today, you can gain a great deal of experience and have a lot of fun. People interested in obedience work are friendly folk, always willing to help and try out new ideas. The more involved you become in the obedience world the more you can enjoy yourself. There are good and bad clubs as well as good and bad trainers, so I would suggest that you attend the club of your choice or the local one if only one exists, and see for yourself if you approve of their methods. A newcomer should attend at least one session without the dog before joining. It can be quite a traumatic experience for both you and the dog, especially a young pup, if you are launched into a totally new set of circumstances; both of you need reassurance, help and instruction, and if you have gained a little first, then you can cope better with your dog.

If at any time you feel a certain test or exercise is beyond the capabilities of you or your dog, then ask the instructor to be excused from taking the floor. Instead quietly watch how others are coping with it and then practise at home. To make a fool of yourself in a class just from sheer bravado does neither you nor the dog any good. Dogs are just as self-conscious as humans and also have the same sense of pride. They hate being laughed at. If the instructor insists that all the dogs in the class perform each exercise in the test and delays the class while trying to persuade a difficult pupil to perform, then join another club. The instructor's duty is to instruct the handler, then the handler should practise at home according to these instructions, and if his homework is correctly done, the class and the pupils will benefit in the following weeks. This is also a world where you must be prepared to see the other person's point of view and accept it. I learned this lesson early on in life and it has stood me in good stead here too. Some trainers and handlers are interested only in getting to the top with a dog trained to perform with the precision of a guardsman, others wish to train only an obedient pet; so much depends upon the personality of the handler.

Border Collies have the reputation of being easy to train, and so they are—but only in the right hands. Some people attending classes who have not had much success with training the first breed they have owned often buy a Border Collie, thinking they are going to have instant success and be the star of the class. They are usually disappointed, as owning a Border Collie for this reason proves that the person has little understanding of the mind of a collie and is therefore unlikely to be any more successful in training than before. If proof of this statement is needed, take note that all the successful collies in a class or test are owned or worked by competent handlers. These dogs are so willing to please, so quick in their actions, that they are good material for the makings of a good obedience worker, but one must also realize that they have minds of their own and must see a reason for obeying any command. Before training can commence you and your collie must build up a trust or partnership; you must get inside his mind and give him confidence that you know what you are doing—only then is training easy. Some collies can never adapt to this form of training as the robot precision that is required and the frustrations of the limited opportunities to work things out for themselves are totally foreign to their nature. In my opinion the line of approach in training a pet collie for obedience work is by gentle but firm commands, being in sympathy with the dog and making sure he has fully understood your requirements from the tone of your voice. If he has understood what you require him to do, yet fails to do it, there is no need for you to punish him. The Border Collie is so sensitive and intelligent that just to let him know you are aware of his failure is almost sufficient punishment in itself; his own sense of guilt will do the rest. Never fail to note too when he has been successful, and praise him accordingly, for this is the only indication you can give him that you are pleased with him. This method does not always succeed in gaining top honours for you and your collie, but it creates a wonderful and worthwhile partnership.

Some people buy a puppy from obedience champion stock, often without sufficient regard to type or temperament, for their main concern is its ability to obey with guardsman-like precision.

These dogs make excellent obedience workers, but are very often totally unreliable outside the ring. This is a situation you rarely find at sheepdog trials. Unfortunately with all forms of competition one gets some element of 'win at any price' in it. They need expert handlers, and I know many of the latter, who can, through understanding, overcome the natural instincts of a collie, mould him into performing obedience test exercises in a natural manner, and end up with a first-class performer and a perfect relationship. I am by no means biased against obedience work. I have been President, Chairman, trainer and general 'mopper-upper' in the world of obedience clubs for over twenty years and know that they give great help and pleasure; but I do not think they use the abilities of their Border Collies to full advantage. Any dog in the right hands can be trained to do these precision obedience tests, but few dogs that do not have some collie blood in their veins can do the work of a sheepdog. The polished performances given by handlers and their dogs at obedience demonstrations and the skill in training is not often appreciated by the general public; it is usually the dog who fails to obey some command who relieves the boredom and gets the biggest response.

Instead of the usual type of demonstration for obedience work put on for the public I should like to see collies giving a demonstration of the work for which they were intended. This could easily be done with the co-operation of a local farmer or smallholder and a few ducks, or, if the venue was suitable, even with two or three geese. Very interesting displays combining obedience and field work are staged by gundog enthusiasts, so why should they not be held for collies as well? In the section of obedience tests which is devoted to outdoor working trials the Border Collies give a very good account of themselves and are excellent tracker dogs. They enjoy these forms of obedience exercises and almost have to be restrained when it comes to competing in the long and high jumping tests. It is interesting that the German shepherd dogs, who do so well at these events, have been tried on various occasions to work with sheep in this country, but they have proved unsatisfactory. However, the German Shepherd will score in other rôles where the Border Collie may fail, and it must be remembered he was bred in his native land to perform his duties in a totally different manner from a collie.

Since 1 May 1976 the Kennel Club have re-named some of the obedience sections. What used to be known as tests now become classes, A, B, C and Ch. Each individual exercise in these classes will be known as a test. Any further information can be obtained from the Kennel Club.

WORKING TRIALS

The same basic obedience exercises are required in this field of training with the addition of those involving tracking, searching and agility, all of which have really practical value for a working dog. To compete in these trials a high degree of skill and expertise is required in both dog and handler, to say nothing of a strong constitution, and weather-resistant coats for both parties. Many a hill collie that has worked over crags and mountain streams, found stray sheep in deep bracken or heather and guided his master home through mist could give a good account of himself at these trials after only a short initiation period.

I have attempted to train one rough and one Border Collie in this field. They both enjoyed the work, excelling in tracking and agility tests, but failed miserably in the search and retrieve tests. They scored full marks for steadiness to gunshot sounds as both had been used on rough shooting expeditions; but when it came to the search I always knew they were looking for game and not for human scents. As a spectator at these trials I am always fascinated by watching or studying the way each breed works, how it approaches each obstacle and in particular the use of the tail and the set of the head of Border Collies when in action. Both are used to great effect. The photographs that I have included of Tessa jumping and tracking, clearly show the positions of the limbs when a collie is in motion (Plates 4b, 12a). The hindquarters perform most of the propulsion, with that extra impetus from the tail, the forequarters and head giving thrust and support to the body. A collie when moving at speed uses every part of the body in perfect harmony. I often wonder if the agility tests entail a lot of extra effort for those breeds with docked tails.

Types of working trials held under Kennel Club rules are at Open and Championship levels, with the following stakes classes:

Companion Dog Stake. (C.D.)

Utility Dog Stake. (U.D.)

Working Dog Stake. (W.D.)

Tracking Dog. (T.D.)

Police Dog. (P.D.)

If a dog gains 70 per cent or more of the points awarded for each stake the initials (i.e. C.D.) may appear after its name. If it gains 80 per cent or more, the word 'Excellent' may also be included. All the stakes include the agility test, which consists of a scale and long jump, the height or length the dog is required to clear to gain full points varying according to the height of the dog. Except in the U.D. stakes, dogs are required to clear the maximum height or length in each of the jumps. The individual tests or exercises both at working trials and sheepdog trials can be seen to be of practical value to a working dog. For those pet owners who are not keen on the strict discipline of the obedience ring or who do not wish to enter the show ring, yet want an interest involving the companionship of their dog I recommend this particular field as a most rewarding experience.

OTHER DUTIES

Because of its adaptability a collie can be trained to do almost anything in the right hands, and this is a point that cannot be stressed too often. It is said that dogs do not have reasoning power, but I feel that a collie could prove this to be wrong. It may not be in the same form as the reasoning power given to humans, but there is no doubt that a collie must see 'the reason why' before he can be convinced of performing the task you set him. He will obey your commands because of his wish to please you, but you and he have got to get together to make a success of further training.

The collie makes a first-class sheepdog because he can see the reason for what he is doing and it is a fairly simple matter for a trainer or handler to put this particular purpose over to the dog. An intelligent, well-trained collie with a novice handler can make quite a good team, especially if the novice is prepared to learn something from the dog and not bend him to his own as yet inefficient ways. The teamwork of handler and collie seen either in the obedience ring at Cruft's, at demonstrations, or on the trials field is the culmination of deep understanding and sympathy together with great experience and, above all, having the right dog in the hands of the right person. The dog has got to suit his handler's personality and none more so than a Border Collie.

Family Pet

Almost daily I am asked if a Border Collie makes a good family pet, and each time my answer is the same—'it depends on the family and the source or parents of the pup'. Unhappily many so-called Border Collies are sold as family pets from very unreliable sources, and of course, whatever breed you buy as a pet, the choice may turn out to be a lucky or unlucky one. If the family have been used to owning a poodle or a Jack Russell terrier, then in my opinion a Border Collie would be an unhappy choice. If, however, they have been used to owning a Labrador or a Beagle, then I feel the qualities of a Border Collie would fit the bill. If you have never owned a dog before, then perhaps when you have read this book you will be in a position to decide if this breed is suitable as your particular family pet. When people come to me to buy a pup as a pet, I can usually tell at once if they are the right type to own a Border Collie. I often find what they really want is a 'Lassie' or rough collie.

With regard to the training of the family pet, basic training begins in the nest, as I explained earlier, so if the pups have been well reared and handled with care and understanding they will already have been started off on the right foot. An untrained dog is a useless nuisance, possibly even a danger, but a trained or obedient dog is a pleasure to own and a source of admiration. Remember that the behaviour of our dogs and their general appearance directly reflect our own characters (see Plate 13b). Basic equipment for training is simple, but aim to buy the best quality— it is the most economical in the long run and will last the dog's life, if not for those that follow as well. While a puppy is growing any cheap old collar will do, as you may need different sizes at the different stages of growth. Some people purchase a choke or check type collar at once and hope it will last the dog's life. I prefer a good quality rounded leather collar with a brass name-plate firmly secured to it. Medals or tags attached to collars tend to wear away at the point of contact and get lost. I have either known or heard of several lost dogs who, when found, had no name on the collar (they sometimes did not even have a collar) and when the owners were eventually traced they swore the collar had a name tag on it.

Getting a puppy accustomed to wearing a collar and then walking on a lead are also very early steps. Where pet dogs are concerned house training is also important. Most puppies would prefer to be clean if only they knew where to deposit their excreta; so it is up to the owner to show the pup where he is expected to perform and then play his part in seeing that it gets to that spot at the correct times. Never pick up a pup and shake it or rub its nose in the dirt if it has misbehaved. Scold it by voice and then show it where it should have deposited it; but better still see that it was put in the right spot at the right time.

May I remind pet owners to make sure that they always address their dogs by calling their name before any command is given. Our dogs hear us talk a great deal, but unless they hear their name, they cannot be expected to know when to react. For example, one often hears a mother out for a walk with her family and their dog saying 'Now children, we will cross the road' or some such remark. The dog is busy sniffing along on his own and suddenly he finds the family have vanished. He is then screamed at and scolded for not complying with a command he was never given—he simply cannot be a mind-reader. The same applies to a dog being trained for any sort of work; always alert the dog first by calling his name and then make sure that he understands the command you are giving is intended for him.

You are the dog's lord and master; his devotion to you can only be expressed in deeds, not words, so make sure you try to repay him with a full understanding of his particular character.

Guarding

Border Collies often adopt the role of children's nanny or family guard. We once had one who adored the sea and boats; he always kept guard on our clothes and on any small toddlers when we went to the beach. Once when we were holidaying on the Norfolk Broads he dived overboard and returned to the bank with a live fish in his mouth. We spent a hazardous half hour trying to get him back on board again, but he refused to drop the fish.

As a child, during some school holidays I used to visit a friend's farm in County Cork and was allowed to take the milk churns to the creamery in one of those donkey carts which are such a familiar feature of the Irish scene. One of the farm collies always accompanied me, running between the wheels under the cart. God help any person or dog who dared to come within a few yards of the entourage! When we got to the creamery I had to tie him up before anyone could get near to off-load the churns. On the way home, if we met a herd of cattle or a flock of sheep being driven in to market, the dog would soon make a passage between them. The old donkey, who could almost have done the journey there and back on his own, would never stop for anything on the return journey, no matter how hard you pulled on the old rope reins. The collie kept me and the cart under constant guard until I went into the house on our return and the donkey was turned out into the field.

Guide Dogs for the Blind

At one time many Border Collies were trained as guide dogs for the blind, but it is a sad reflection that because so many of the wrong type were given to the Association for training they are no longer used unless one outstanding pup comes forward; also, the fact that Border Collies are now being bred so much smaller than collies in the past, creates a height problem when in harness.

Mountain Rescue

The Search and Rescue Dog Association was started by Hamish MacInnes of Glencoe in 1965 after he had attended a course in Switzerland. In 1971 the Association split into separate groups covering England, Scotland and Wales. Two founder members were the Elliott brothers, hill farmers from Glencoe who trained their working collies for this very important task. The family have been famous for their services to mountain rescue for a very long time.

The Alsatian (or German Shepherd Dog) is the breed mostly used in mountain rescue work, but quite a few Border Collies are giving good accounts of themselves; the choice of dog remains with the handler, and there are many who find the collie admirably suitable, particularly on steep slopes where a bigger dog is at a great disadvantage. A further point in the collie's favour is his aptitude for being able to work far away from his handler, thereby covering a very large area of ground while picking up human scent, leaving less ground for the handler to cover and saving precious time. For my part, if I was lying injured in a gulley I would feel comforted at once by the sight of a Border Collie.

It is interesting that a dark-haired dog is less susceptible to snow-blindness. The coat must be weather-resistant, so the good old-fashioned Highland Collie from whom the Border Collie is descended, should be the ideal dog for the job. The distinctive coat worn by the mountain rescue dogs is their badge of office and is made up of reflective material to enable them to be picked up by torchlight at night. Often a collar with bells attached is worn, which also assists in keeping track of the dog at night or in thick mist. This all sounds very reminiscent of the tales of those old shepherds in bygone days who relied on their dogs to guide them home. These dogs often wore bells on their collars and their white markings were picked up by the lantern light.

Handlers are enlisted from people involved in mountain rescue in the mountain and moorland regions of the United Kingdom. For open country searchwork and in avalanche techniques an annual four-day training course is held during the first three months of the year, at which novice dogs receive training and assessment, and trained dogs are reassessed. The dogs working off the airborne scent of the victim must be able to find him and then indicate his whereabouts to the handler. All dogs are vetted before being enrolled for an initial course, the first requirement being a good standard in basic obedience tests. There is then a livestock test to ensure that they will not worry other animals, with a specific test in a pen of sheep, which the dogs must pass before being accepted, and they are also carefully scrutinized throughout the course in this respect.

Dogs are graded into categories relative to each year of training and the standard attained, and each handler is issued with a certificate stating the grade the dog has attained. Grade C is awarded to the dog for life and there is also a Certificate of Merit which can be awarded to any dog which finds a victim in a real search.

There is no charge for the services provided by the Association, these being met by the handlers themselves, but equipment is supplied. The Association does indeed provide a wonderful service, and only the dogs make it possible.

Tracking

Border Collies are used for tracking, not just in the course of arresting criminals but for locating lost children, valuables, and even for scenting out drugs. In the latter case, the collie has the advantage of size over the German Shepherd Dog when working in confined spaces like warehouses or aircraft. This is a limited and specialized form of work and is distinct from the tracking at working trials. I have written about many other of these exploits, such as stage performances and the rôle Border Collies have played in both World Wars in my previous book. Suffice it to say here that a Border Collie can be relied upon to give a good account of himself and even to reach top honours, in whatever field he has been properly trained.

THE SHOW RING

A farmer would not send his livestock exhibit to Smithfield Show or elsewhere without at least halter-training it, and presenting it either washed or groomed according to the requirements of each animal; nor would anyone present a working hunter in the show ring without ensuring it is well-groomed and trained in ring manners, and it is just as necessary to train and groom a dog for this purpose. Show qualities in the animal are of course the first essentials, but it is difficult for a novice to assess these qualities until he has seen the animal in competition with others and has learned the finer points of the breed requirements, both from a study of the exhibits or from talking to judges and other exhibitors. Good presentation and ring behaviour, or good handling, can sometimes hoodwink a judge into thinking an animal is better than it really is, and only a fool would not try to take advantage of this situation, although most judges know their job too well to be taken in; still, presenting your exhibit to its best advantage may help to tip the scales in your favour when the opposition is stiff. In my experience a dog intended for the show ring should not be taught strict obedience exercises until he has had some experience in the ring, as he will learn to walk too close to the handler and sit when required to stand. It is often argued that a well-trained dog can be taught to perform both in the obedience ring and the show ring. This is correct up to a point, but can only be attempted by experienced handlers, and there are very few dogs capable of winning well in both rings.

Regarding the actual showing of dogs, the psychological or therapeutic effect this form of sport or hobby can have on the lives of different people has not been sufficiently acknowledged. I have always been interested in people as much as in their dogs. I have watched lonely or handicapped men and women, broken-hearted couples, and even sheer 'bad hats' become completely transformed and derive the utmost pleasure from being able to show their dogs and get involved in all the activities that surround the show world.

In my final chapter I have given fuller details and information on showing a collie, but no amount of reading will compensate for actual experience gained at classes or in the ring. The conclusions I have drawn from the various theories on training put forward by experienced handlers is that it is important first to decide for what purpose we are training the dog and then only to train to the stage which both the dog and handler are capable of attaining. I am of the opinion that the training of a dog for sheepwork is more highly skilled than for any other purpose.

Chapter 3

SHEEPDOG TRIALS

The development of sheepdog trials is possibly the most important part in the story of the evolution and popularity of the modern Border Collie. I will deal first with the background and teamwork employed in organizing modern sheepdog trials.

The objectives of the trials are threefold. First, to provide an arena for testing the working ability of sheepdogs in order to assess their potential for future breeding and the better management of sheep. Second, to create a form of competition involving all the skills in the ancient art of shepherding. Third, to give members of the public the only opportunity of witnessing at close range the skills of these dogs and the men that handle them, which are by no means the most important part of shepherding, but appear as the most exacting to the observer.

Each trial schedules different classes of varying standards at either local, national or international level, which in turn cater for either the hired shepherd, farmer or flockmaster (see new ruling on page 100). Competition at international level is a team event for competitors who have gained the necessary qualifications at national level. For those who are interested I give fuller explanations later.

The atmosphere surrounding sheepdog trials is akin to that of a sports stadium or open air theatre and in this context I propose to study the roles of the promoters, producers and performers, before embarking upon the story of how these events started.

The promoters are usually local sheepdog societies, or firms connected with agriculture; sometimes county agricultural shows include sheepdog demonstrations in their Grand Ring programme as an added attraction. Since its formation in 1906 the International Sheep Dog Society has been responsible for promoting most of these trials, and in 1922 when Wales joined they started the national and international trials.

The production team consists of either select committees or working parties who are responsible for every detail regarding the smooth running of the trials at any level. Their praises often go unsung, yet they are the backbone of any society. Their tasks include finding suitable venues not only for the actual course but one that has easy access in and out, plus parking areas for cars and caravans. Vets, the National Farmers' Union and Ministry of Agriculture officials have all to be contacted, not to mention local press and police. Availability of hotel and other accommodation is another of their problems, as are the catering and other facilities on the course. Supplies of sheep must be laid on—these are just a very few of the important tasks undertaken by these 'production or stage managers'. Following them are the course planners and directors, stewards, and people to man gates and sell programmes and so on; these all come within the scope of this team. Secretaries and their staff are present at all stages to direct and to watch the plans on their office drawing board taking shape on the field. Now and again the best laid plans can be upset even at the eleventh hour by an outbreak of foot and mouth disease or something similar, and an alternative plan has to be put into action. I believe there have been several occasions when even a third plan has had to be considered. At local level it is very disappointing when a trial has to be cancelled; at national level alternative sites are a headache; but at international level it could reach disaster proportions. However, in the history of the International Sheep Dog Society only wars have so far defeated the organizers in their tasks.

Of the main performers in the arena I will deal first with the *sheep*, which are usually supplied by local farmers; their character and performance can be guaranteed to be the determining factor in the success or failure of each trial. The sheep await their turn in the wings and enter the arena in groups of three, five or ten, or as the type of competition demands. Years ago wild hill or mountain sheep were often specially imported into a district, if the trials were being held in a part of the country where the local sheep were mainly folded, as it was believed these local sheep were too heavy, tame or sluggish to give a good performance. I have seen some wonderfully spirited performances by real wild hill sheep at trials in the Border counties of England, and also in Wales. Even in the south of England the sheep can sometimes be very unco-operative. Anyone owning a dog of any variety can enter for local trials provided the dog is trained to run, but at trials under International Sheep Dog Society rules the dogs must be registered with the Society to be eligible for competition. Handlers taking part at any level may come from other walks of life beside farmers, hired shepherds or flockmasters. Likely lads with dogs of very doubtful parentage, sportsmen with gundog types and many others made up the list of competitors in the past. Today the standard of competition is so high that those who enter while running their dogs only as a hobby stand little chance of high honours, if that is their aim. Knowledge of sheep and their ways besides having a well-trained dog is essential if a handler wants to get and to give maximum pleasure.

Speaking from my own experience, the handlers I have been privileged to know and talk with, are all modest reticent men of high principles, with that special quality of humility that belongs to people with a vast knowledge and understanding of their art. Whilst these are admirable qualities that I greatly appreciate, by their very nature they have made my task of researching both frustrating and difficult.

To the observant and dedicated spectator, a handler's whole character and personality becomes apparent from the moment he steps under the ropes on to the course. Even the type of clothes he wears, the angle of his cap, or the way he calls his dog, makes it possible for a keen spectator like myself to recognize the competitor at the post without consulting the programme or hearing his number announced.

I may have given the impression that this is an all-male pursuit, but let me at once correct this. A few ladies do compete from time to time, and in 1977 Miss Jean Hardisty won the English National Trials, then captained the English team at the International Trials. History was made as she was the first woman to do so. It was a real triumph, and Jean, an accountant, does all the training of her dog Flash in her spare time.

The star performers are the dogs themselves, and in fact they can also be amongst the keenest of spectators. Some just go to sleep while awaiting their turn; others follow every move of their rivals. Here I would like to try to dispel a theory held by many that dogs run in trials are in some way just specialist dogs kept solely for this purpose. Criticism comes only from those who do not fully understand the qualities required for this type of performance, and in consequence one also hears it said that 'trials-bred' dogs are useless for hill or farm work. For their basic training alone the dogs must be capable of carrying out normal routine work and this is actually exactly what they do each day when not competing. A good hill dog who runs well when out of sight, working out his own line in his own time, may be quite useless to run in trials where he must work more closely with his master over a definite restricted course in a limited time. However dependable he may be when running on the hills, this type of work will not suit him. Equally, the timid dog or the one who dislikes other dogs, strange situations or hordes of humans may be totally unsuited to run at trials while being indispensable on the hirsel or farm. It will, then, be appreciated that far from being useless, these 'trials-bred' dogs are in fact super-stars and possess not only the capabilities for routine work, but that extra intelligence and willing temperament to warrant the higher standard of training needed for this type of display. In these days stars at any public performance and the people behind the scenes as well, get vast sums of money for their appearance, whereas here we have all the main characters and the stars giving their services free, except for out of pocket expenses in a few cases. Although financial rewards do follow both for societies and competitors in the form of gate money or from the progeny and stud fees from top winners, this is not the object of the operation. Fees are of course charged by individual people giving specific types of demonstrations (these fees are quite often later donated to charity), but that is a private matter between the persons concerned.

Apart from a society newsletter or magazine very little credit is publicly given to all the wonderful volunteers who stage the trials for us every year in spite of the ever-increasing difficulties being encountered. They give so much pleasure and create one of the best means of getting town and country folk together without any of the ingredients for stirring up mass hysteria or hooliganism.

EARLY HISTORY OF TRIALS

Even in the old droving days, whenever men and their dogs gathered together either for some special task connected with their flock or simply for relaxation, some form of competition or wager was seen to emerge at a certain stage of the proceedings, and in particular at dipping and shearing times, or at the fairs. Each man that came to help brought his own dog or dogs who were trained for specific tasks with their flocks, and friendly rivalry as to whose dog would perform these tasks best would always end in various forms of competitions which later became an established part of rural life known as 'collie gatherings'. As these became more and more popular, members of the public and the owners of the estates where they were held became increasingly upset at the unkempt appearance and divergence of type of the dogs taking part. It was then that the decision to change the name to sheepdog trials or gatherings came into force, mainly to avoid trouble when objections were lodged. It was hoped eventually to encourage the breeding of a purer strain of dog for sheep work, by a process of selection, and in order to distinguish them from the collie or useful farm dog of the day. This was a very important step and the first indication we have of this distinction. At first the classes were for collies, but due to the divergence of types entered the wording of the classes was changed to 'any dog irrespective of his strain so long as he is properly trained and broken to sheep work may compete'.

My biggest breakthrough in my quest for details on early trials came from a book lent to me by a friend. It was *The Collie or Sheepdog* by Rawdon B. Lee. I already had a copy of this book, but did not feel it contributed much that was new to me, until my friend's copy turned up. This one had belonged to the Rev. Hans Hamilton, a great collie fancier and a man also concerned with pastoral life at the grass roots. He had marked or corrected in his own handwriting several of the passages in his copy. Lee was a great lover of dogs and wrote several books on the subject. He was also editor of the *Kendal Mercury* until 1883 and then became Kennel Editor of *The Field* until 1907. He was known to his colleagues as a rather verbose gentleman given to many inaccuracies in his reporting, hence Hamilton's remarks and alterations, or so one might conclude. It seems that letters of protest regarding the appearance and general condition or treatment of the collies littered the desks of these men and of many others in public life at the time. It was therefore decided, in addition to the other alterations for these meetings, to make an award for the best turned-out or conditioned dog competing at what were by then being called sheepdog meetings.

Good relationships between tenants and landlords, particularly those with sporting interests, are essential in a rural community; so too are the relationships between shepherds and gamekeepers, especially in the matter of their dogs' individual abilities. Owners of large sporting estates in the Border counties between England and Wales were the first to become interested in this new form of exhibition, of which the Victorians were so proud—namely, dog shows. So when tests and field trials for gundogs became the vogue all the facilities for such functions were there on the spot; above all there was the railway, which provided a more rapid form of transport than in the past.

These trials grew from one- to three-day events. In order to maintain cordial relations between landlords and the shepherds who were being inconvenienced on such occasions, the organizers decided to devote the third day to holding trials for the shepherds' dogs. Once again all the facilities and arrangements for such events were on the spot. The first event where birds were driven and the dogs shot over, was on 10 and 11 September 1867. This meeting was held on the 64,000-acre Rhwylas estate of Richard Lloyd Price, near Bala in North Wales, but three-day events were not held for another six years. Meantime a great deal of experience was gained in the organizing of such events, so that by the time the first public sheepdog trials were staged everything was to hand to ensure its success. Mr Price was a well-known breeder of gundogs and later of Old English Sheepdogs, but it was his friend Mr S. E. Shirley from over the border in Gloucestershire, himself a well-known collie and gundog breeder, who later persuaded him to extend the trials to sheepdogs. In fact in October 1873, together with Mr Parmeter and Mr Ellis, these two men organized the whole three-day event, and Mr Shirley founded the Kennel Club that same year.

A considerable amount of publicity was given in the popular county journals to these events, so by that date they had become a major rural attraction and with the addition of sheepdog competitions their popularity was assured; in fact this particular event attracted a crowd of 300 spectators with ten shepherds competing. Besides the prize for the winner of the trial, an extra trophy was offered for the most handsome dog competing. The same dog won both awards, Tweed, a collie from Scotland belonging to a Scots shepherd, James Thompson, who was working in Wales at the time. The report on the trials written for *The Field* by R. L. Price, whom I presume was the promoter himself, or his son, was almost as noteworthy as the event itself. A friend and I received the kind permission of *The Field* to look into their archives and found the article, which is too long to quote here, amusing and atmospheric. It gives splendid descriptions of the penning and driving trials, and of Tweed's unmatched skill. Despite the torrential rain and the occasional instance of sheep mingling with the crowd, there is no doubt from Mr Price's account that the trials were received with immense enthusiasm.

Following the success of these trials others were held in the Principality at Garth and Llangollen, and in 1875 they returned to Bala where this time there were over 2,000 spectators and thirty-five competitors. The Bala trials grew more and more popular and in 1878 they merged with Llangollen. The first trials held in England were at Byrness in 1876. History does not recount who organized them, but the winner was Walter Telfer, from Northumberland. Scotland held its first trials at Carnwath the same year, the winner being James Gardener from North Cobbinshaw. Both these men contributed in no small measure to the improvement of the breed and both were exemplary characters and true experts in their art. The Rev. Hamilton has noted against the paragraph in Lee's book on the above trials that a special trials committee was formed to undertake the arrangements and preliminaries. I wonder if that committee could be regarded as the first to run these events or even possibly to have formed the first Sheepdog Society or Association. One other paragraph regarding trials where he had placed a stroke and a question mark in the margin was when the writer referred to classes at trials for puppies, which reads as follows: 'Arrangements are generally made by which the puppies, that have a special stake for themselves, work over a shorter and easier course than the all-aged dogs, for reasons that will naturally be obvious.' The only comment I have to make here is that these old-time handlers must have been very clever or the pups very forward to get them up to that standard of training while still under twelve months of age.

In 1889 Queen Victoria and other members of the Royal Family visited the Llangollen course and this gave sheepdog trials a great boost. The Queen was very fond of collies and owned several, exhibiting some of them at the early shows. During the royal visit the organizer of the trials that year, Captain Best, also arranged some special sheepdog displays by several noted handlers from all over Wales and parts of Lancashire. Several years later some readers' letters to *The Field* containing criticisms of sheepdog trials were replied to by Captain Best and others who had staged many trials in different parts of Britain. These letters provided me with much information on these events. The earliest mention I found of societies promoting or organizing trials was in 1878 when the North Western Counties Sheepdog Trials Association was formed. Others were held at Oswestry, Llanberis and Silecroft.

While still on the subject of the early history of these events, present-day course planners may be amused by the advice in a little leaflet I found called 'Recommendations for setting out a course', and I quote the following from it: 'A trial ground should not be level like a racecourse; it is better more or less undulating; with a footpath or two running across; a dry burn or ghyll to pass over; a gap or opening in a fence or hedge to be driven through. Roughish land is best of all, even if it lay along a hillside.' I wonder if anyone has yet found this ideal course and if so whether they have thought of providing ponies or helicopters for the spectators, and a T.V. camera platform for the judges!

Let me give you a brief description of exercises undertaken by the competitors at trials before the societies took over and laid down rules and guidelines. The courses were very much as described above, being a fairly accessible stretch of countryside preferably with a hillside flanking it somewhere as a good view-point for spectators. The descriptions of some early trials mention that the competitor was required to hold on to a piece of rope, throughout the drive which was attached to the starting post. I presume that this was so that he would be unable to help the dog. Others mention that it was the dog that had to be held to the post by the piece of rope until the signal was given to start the drive. Sheep in the holding area came from two or three different farms. When released, three at a time, two were from the same farm and one from another, and here the fun began. The sheep were to be driven on a course marked by flags and through, over or around all the obstacles mentioned, for a distance of about three-quarters of a mile in depth and extending over several fields. The drive, with the one odd sheep which usually refused to join the others, had its share of incidents. All three would disappear the wrong

1a.   Type of dish found most suitable for feeding puppies from weaning to approximately eight weeks. *Owner:* the author. (*Photo:* Photovogue)

1b.   Puppies should always be introduced to stock on a lead and preferably in the company of an older and quieter dog. *Owner:* the author. (*Photo:* G. B. Royffé, A.R.P.S.)

2a. Obedience Champion, Stillmoor Jamie of Hurstview. *Owner:* Paula Lister. (*Photo:* John Wright)

2b. International Sheepdog Champion, Gel. *Owner:* H. L. Jones. (*Photo:* Chris Birchall, L.R.P.S.)

3a.   Glen, the farm or cattle dog. *Owner:* H. J. Jones. (*Photo:* Chris Birchall, L.R.P.S.)

3b.   Guide dog for the blind. A fully qualified collie in harness.
(*Photo:* Nicholas Toyne)

4a. Bryn, a search and rescue collie. *Owner:* David Riley, Honorary Secretary of the English branch of the Search and Rescue Dog Association based in Cumbria. (*Photo:* David Longford)

4b. Working Trials Champion, Tessa of Thornymoor. *Owner:* Doris Cowley. (*Photo:* Frank Garwood)

5a. Shep with John Noakes of BBC Television's 'Blue Peter' fame. (*Photo:* BBC TV)

5b. 'On Guard' by William Weekes. Gamekeeper and shepherd often combined occupations; note the gun and water bottle in the foreground. The typical collie of the Border counties is lying on the shepherd's plaid or rug.

6a. 'In From Sport' by George Armfield. Both the English setter and the spaniels of this period were not unlike the old-type collies in appearance.

6b. A modern registered Border Collie as seen in the obedience ring. Note a similarity to these gun dogs even today. *Owner:* Hugh Rose. (*Photo:* D. L. Clarke)

7a. 'Dorset Sheepdog' by T. S. Cooper.

7b. 'Sussex Sheepdog' by T. S. Cooper. Most of the old droving and farming dogs were of this type. An interesting feature is the Pyecombe hook; the making of these was a thriving industry at one time in the district.

8a. Queen, one of the
best bitches ever produced
in England.

8b. Fingland Loos, the
mother of champions Fly,
Nell, Roy and Nickey.

9a. Old Kep, Troneyhill's most famous collie.

9b. Hemp, one of the most famous sires and Number 9 in the Stud Book.

10a. Old Maid, the
Number 1 entry in the
I.S.D.S. Stud Book.

BROWN, ANDREW, Boghall, Oxton, Lauder.

No. 1. OLD MAID. Bitch. Smooth. B. & W. —/—/—.
Sire :—Don (A. Renwick).
Dam :—Nell (T. P. Brown).

10b. The companion
dog. The combined
ages of the man and
his dogs in this group
add up to 104 years of
happiness. (*Photo:* Ron
Hawksbee)

11a.   A collie in perfect charge of her flock. (*Photo:* G. B. Royffé, A.R.P.S.)

11b.   Counting sheep on the marshes. The collies will keep the lots apart and cut out any particular sheep if required. (*Photo:* Ron Hawksbee)

11c.   A demonstration of penning in Northumberland. (*Photo:* Hylton Edgar)

12a. A good type of male and female Border Collie now living in retirement. (*Photo:* Photovogue)

12b. The late Willie Wallace demonstrating sheepdog handling in its highest form, with his eight Border Collies which he worked together as a team using separate whistles for each dog. One dog in the team was totally blind. (*Photo:* London Express)

13a. A good illustration of the way to train a young puppy for the correct position of dog and handler in the show ring. (*Photo:* G. B. Royffé, A.R.P.S.)

13b. The behaviour and general appearance of our dogs directly reflect our own character. (*Photo:* Ron Hawksbee)

14a. A bitch feeding her pups from the standing position as in the latter stages of lactation. (*Photo:* Photovogue)

14b. Tessa seen taking a long jump. This shows clearly the position of the limbs of a collie in motion and the extra impetus given by the tail. (*Photo:* Surrey Advertiser)

15a and b. Two good working types. In each case note the extra long tibia bones and excellent set of tails, essential to good moving and turning at high speed. (*Photos:* Ron Hawksbee)

16. The appeal of a Border Collie. (*Photo:* Bertram Unné, A.I.B.P., A.R.P.S.)

way up the footpath, or the so-called dry ghyll would then be a rushing stream due to a storm in the hills, or the wrong gap was found in the hedge. However, out of sight of the judges and to avoid admission payment, local lads or children could be counted on to persuade any unwilling sheep to swim the burn or go through the right gap. Indeed, as a child I was guilty of taking part in just such a manoeuvre though fortunately I was not caught. The dogs seemed to expect it of us. These misguided pranks did not always have the desired effect and on one occasion some of my friends in the gang were very sore in a certain place for several days after causing one old man to be disqualified.

Finally the dog was required to pen his sheep in the same way as he does today. I have often seen dogs being required to put the sheep through a set of hurdles in the form of a Maltese Cross. This exercise was later dropped except for demonstrations at shows; it was regarded as too much like a circus act and too time-consuming when trying to get wild mountain sheep through such an unusual obstacle. Welsh societies were the prime movers in its abolition. Its original purpose was to test the ability of a dog to push its sheep through a narrow gap or a sheep dip.

This may be an appropriate place to record an incident regarding the formation of one of these societies which were now taking over the running of trials from private enterprises. It concerns a shepherd and a gamekeeper who, it is claimed, were responsible for starting the Longshaw Sheepdog Trials Society in March 1898, as the result of a bet. The Duke of Rutland's gamekeeper, Ellis Ashton, boasted that he could shoot more pigeons from a trap than Ernest Priestly, a local sheep farmer, and he suggested that they should have a friendly competition to prove the point. To the gamekeeper's fury the farmer won and for revenge he at once proposed a return shoot, as he guessed the farmer did not have a gun licence. So he planned to have a policeman appear on the scene during the shoot. Someone tipped off the farmer and when the policeman appeared Ernest told him, 'I have neither gun nor licence and I don't want to borrow a gun again, but I'll tell you what I'll do. We will have a dog trial to see whose dog can round up sheep the best and I'll give a fat sheep as first prize.' No prizes for guessing who won, but history relates that afterwards the Duke of Rutland presented a Gold Cup to the first organized trials of the society.

The newly formed Kennel Club was persuaded by some collie exhibitors to stage trials for those enthusiasts who wished to try to prove that the show collie was equal to its country cousin. Alexandra Palace was the chosen venue and the year was 1876. Great publicity had been given to the event and a hundred sheep were brought specially by road and train from Mr Price's Rhywlas estate in Wales and were accompanied by one of his shepherds. They arrived in excellent condition and were duly penned in the Palace grounds. Those responsible for planning the course had little idea of the special requirements, or so it is recorded, and the handlers had more enthusiasm than experience. The object of the exercise was to try to dispel the growing belief that the show collie was losing its ability to work, through breeding and lack of practice. The whole event was more like a game of hide and seek than a sheepdog trial. Sheep, once released, bolted off in all directions with dogs in hot pursuit. Many left the parkland and headed for the gardens, darting round and round the rose beds, finally taking refuge behind the shrubberies. There were some very red faces by the end of the day and all those concerned said 'never again'. However, there was at least one collie to complete the course, and Mr J. Thomas's red bitch Madie was declared the winner. The entire exercise was of course a dismal failure, and I have often wondered if it was the Kennel Club or some other party who was responsible for the cost of mounting such an event.

The above report came from a collie magazine of that year, but it differs somewhat from the impression given in a photograph which appeared in the International Sheep Dog Society Centenary souvenir programme of the Bala Trials in 1973; here dogs and handlers appeared to be of the true shepherding fraternity, yet the winner in both reports is given as John Thomas. The caption of the I.S.D.S. photograph reads: 'The first Colley Trials (sequel to the first Bala Trials) Alexandra Park London 30th June 1876.'

98

This is indeed confusing and one wonders if the winner was in fact that same shepherd from Rhywlas, as the second report stated he came from Bala—or was he some other Welshman? If so this would prove my point that the competitor who knows the ways of sheep has a distinct advantage here. Neither description is of direct consequence now, but they do explain just one area where inaccurate reporting has made the task of students like myself very difficult and has caused many wrong impressions regarding the breed.

History repeated itself almost a hundred years later when the trophy won by John Thomas on that day in 1876, was presented again at the International Trials in Bala in 1973. I am of the opinion that possibly there were two trials, one following the other (the date of the latter being given as 30 June); one being run by Mr Price and the other by the Kennel Club, but we shall never know now for certain, and it does not matter, for both reports have given us food for thought and a lesson to be learned.

ONE HUNDRED YEARS ON

Just as a group of far-sighted men got together in 1873 to form the Kennel Club, which was to act as a governing body in affairs appertaining to show dogs, so too did a group of men assemble in 1906 to form a society to control and administer the affairs of the shepherding world. This group, mostly Scotsmen, met at Haddington in Scotland to form the International Sheep Dog Society. I have described its objectives earlier in this book. How better to make the aims of the Society known than to hold a trial where the greatest number of interested folk could be gathered together? So the first 'International' trial was held in Scotland in the same year, 1906, at Gullane near Edinburgh. It was a one-day event, but resulted in enrolling a hundred new members for a subscription of 2s. 6d. per annum.

The activities of the Society were confined to Scotland for several years, but one of its purposes, as its very name implies, was eventually to extend its activities all over these islands wherever help was needed. There can be little doubt that through the years the various officials and many individual members of the Society have helped immensely in improving the whole art of shepherding and encouraging the breeders and trainers of sheepdogs to achieve the standard of excellence they enjoy today. Particular credit must go to James Reid, its Secretary for thirty-two years and the founder of the Stud Book, which is of great benefit to the new generation of breeders. I have given more details regarding this matter in Chapter 1.

Some of the fun and light-hearted atmosphere of those olden days when men of the same interests met together, still exists today at trials, and there is a wonderful spirit of camaraderie among the competitors. However, as with all competitive events, there must be rules and regulations for the benefit of all concerned, and this is where the International Sheep Dog Society plays its full part in making the trials as fair as possible, always, of course, taking human error into account. When attending Society meetings one might almost be forgiven for thinking that it was concerned exclusively with trials; but these are only part of the work.

The dedicated trials spectator and competitor and any member of the International Sheep Dog Society will be fully acquainted with the growth of the various tests and the regulations for entry for present-day trials; having studied their development over a period of almost a hundred years in the previous chapter we will proceed to examine the development during this century of the new and improved strain of collie taking part that was emerging as a direct result of the efforts of the local societies or associations. This new strain used to be referred to as 'trial-bred' collies and had their share of criticism from some quarters, but the demand both at home and abroad for the progeny from trials winners far exceeded the supply. It was felt at one time that farmers and flockmasters had more time and better opportunity for training their dogs than the hired shepherd, so the Society held separate classes for hired shepherds. But 'the times they are a-changing' and in 1976 it was decided to abolish these separate classes as modern conditions in farm work now make it possible for all to compete on equal terms. At the time, however, it was considered a great step forward and also increased the membership when the International Sheep Dog Society decided to schedule separate classes at trials for hired shepherds. When the International Sheep Dog Society was formed it was regarded only as another Sheepdog Society with a rather ambiguous title, and a move such as this, and another in 1927 when the events were extended to two days, with preliminary trials on the first day to weed out those dogs not up to standard, was popular and again brought increased membership. In 1919 there were only three championships to be won at these trials, the Supreme Overall Champion, the Farmer's Champion and the Shepherd's Champion. Prior to that date there was only one competition. Then in 1927 a team contest was introduced and 1929 was the first brace contest; in 1937 the Driving Championship was introduced.

When James Reid founded the Stud Book he wanted to revert to the old name 'collie' since the reason for changing it to the name of 'sheepdog' in the last century was now no longer necessary. He gave the name 'Border Collie' to this new strain, as it was the dogs from the Border counties between England and Scotland that formed the foundation stock. However, as the Society had 'sheepdog' in its title and it was permissible to have any type of dog entered in the Stud Book provided it could be proved that it had sufficient working ability to warrant merit, the name remained, but the words 'Border Collie' were inserted in brackets on the application form. One further innovation crept in during this century, namely, referring to the competitors as handlers; this is, of course, correct since not all competitors are shepherds or farmers, but somehow—to me at any rate—it smacks of the obedience ring.

This is not the place for detailed reference to societies or trials outside the United Kingdom, but in many parts of the world the history of both is similar to ours. Sheepdog trials are held in many countries of the world. Requirements and conditions differ and in some cases the tests for the dogs are even more severe, laying particular stress on certain qualities. Once you have embarked upon such a fascinating subject as this it is difficult to know at which point to call a halt as it has so many interesting facets. I have tried to confine myself chiefly to the general areas concerning the collies which by this time were being regarded as Border Collies, rather than exclusively in their role as sheepdogs and in the context of trials.

In J. Herries McCulloch's book *Sheepdogs and their Masters*, published in 1938 (now alas, out of print), there is a wonderful chapter entitled 'Carnival of Champions'. He describes sheepdog trials as 'a festival of honest shepherds and their honest dogs and in mingling with them it is impossible not to be brought back to a sense of rugged reality'. In another delightful sentence he writes of the Trials 'they bring the flavour of the hills to jaded city nostrils'. At the back of the book he gives a most excellent geneaological chart of supreme champion winners of International Sheep Dog Society Trials from 1906 to 1937, tracing their ancestry back to Hemp. I only wish I could include just such a chart here, but whereas Mr McCulloch's work covered a period of only thirty years, today I would have to add the records of a further forty years to this list. To do full justice to these dogs and to the men who bred and trained them would require a whole book on the subject. Perhaps someone with a complete set of Stud Books will take up this challenge.

However, I do not feel that this book would be complete without reference to at least some outstanding trials-winning dogs of the past who have contributed to the breed, besides Telfer's Hemp, whom I have described earlier, and later Dickson's Hemp. During my researches three collies have claimed my attention more than any others. Of these three the first is Kep, later known as Auld Kep, regarded as the Tronyhill's most famous collie. He was said to be a finely coupled dog of the Border Collie type with a strong 'eye'. Bred from Snowdon's Spot and Turner's Cleg, he was purchased by James Scott of Hawick when he was almost a year old, who declared him to be 'one of the great dogs of history'. He won the International in 1908 and 1909 and sired numerous winning sons and daughters, the most famous being Moss who won the International in 1907 and was owned by William Wallace, who later exported him to a Mr Lilico in New Zealand; his name was changed to Border Boss, but unfortunately the move changed his luck as he failed to make much impression at trials out there. There is an old country saying 'change the name, change the luck' and one I ardently subscribe to, being of a superstitious nature.

The next outstanding collie that claimed my attention was Fingland Loos. She was said to be 'the greatest bitch in the modern history of the breed'. This of course referred to the pre-1940 period. She was bred by James Reid who claimed she was the 'best sheep bitch that ever lived'. Reid owned both her sire, Telfers Laddie, and her dam, another Loos, and she was sold to William Wallace of Fingland fame at eight months old, hence her prefix. She later won many championships but above all she passed on her greatest abilities to her sons and daughters, including Dickson's Nickey who was later exported to Mr Lilico in New Zealand. She was also the dam of Wilson's Champions Fly, Nell, and Roy, a winner of three international championships. She died in 1937 at the age of sixteen years.

Queen was the third notable collie to catch my eye in the records, chiefly because of her startled appearance, large ears and her almost hypnotic 'eye'. She won many championships, including the International in 1932. Owned by Walter Telfer, she was by Glending's Ben out of Scott's Maddie. It was claimed that she was 'one of the best bitches ever produced in England'. Ill luck robbed her of top honours on two occasions, and a few years later, in 1938, a Mr C. T. Allen of Cardiff presented a cup at the Southport Trials to be won outright by the unluckiest competitor of the day, named the Hard Luck Cup.

I feel I should mention the trials that have taken place in London during this century, bringing a breath of the countryside to the capital. Many wonderful demonstrations were given at Wembley, but the most famous were those held for many years in Hyde Park, sponsored by the *Daily Express*. Being held during the Easter weekend they became an extremely popular feature in the London calendar of events. They had to be discontinued due to the very high cost of staging them, but not before their fame had spread to many parts of the world through the thousands of overseas visitors who watched them spell-bound each year. Bringing country pursuits to town is a rewarding endeavour as it encourages town folk to visit the country and to appreciate this association as part of our heritage.

Nor could I conclude this chapter without mention of the two recently very popular BBC television series 'One Man and His Dog'. These were specially organized trials with eight handlers and their dogs competing for a 'Television Trophy' presented by the BBC. The first series was filmed in the Lake District beside the superb lake setting of Buttermere. In my opinion no professional team of men and dogs could have given a more thrilling and polished performance during the three days on location there. It was estimated that over four million viewers watched the programmes; each series ended with a brace competition, and finally the winners of each series met to decide the supreme team of man and dog. We were guided through each movement of man and dog with a most enlightening commentary by Eric Halsall, that North Country expert on Sheepdog pedigrees and records. He would have us on the edges of our chairs with remarks like 'great stuff this, grand shepherding', thus allowing the uninitiated to appreciate to the full a particularly skilled performance by experts in the art. Indeed, it is to him and to Archie McDiarmid, that impressive past Chairman of the International Sheep Dog Society, that I owe a great debt of gratitude for their help with regard to the Stud Book and Society records mentioned in this chapter. I have also had a great deal of help in matters relating to the Society from its past Secretary, Lance Alderson, but his researches on my behalf were hampered by lack of records due to a disastrous fire in the office of their previous headquarters, so we had to rely on the long memories of the older generation of trialists.

PRESENT-DAY TRIALS

To compete at trials is a pleasure reserved for the very few, but to watch them is a pleasure we can all enjoy. I suppose one might almost call this a spectator sport, rather in the same category as greyhound racing or horse trials, for each provides entertainment and relaxation for the spectator and acts as a testing ground for the breeds. This aspect of the Border Collie is as complex as any other, so before setting the scene for the present-day sheepdog trial I feel I must break the subject down into sections by covering the parts played by the spectators, competitors and dogs, in that order.

Being a dedicated spectator, whenever family commitments permit I steal away for a couple of days and try to visit as many trials as possible during the season. My husband rarely accompanies me on these trips; he prefers to watch the 'cream on the top' at the internationals. But local trials are my favourites, as I like to follow through the fortunes of beginner dogs from this level upwards. Whenever possible I stay at one of those welcoming bed and breakfast farmhouses, where the bedrooms are adequate and the breakfasts superb. For me, part of the fun is absorbing the local atmosphere by chatting to the owners or having a meal at the local pub. In this way I often meet other dedicated spectators or overseas visitors touring the district who in consequence have often decided to include in their itinerary a visit to the trials. Several have written to me afterwards saying that the experience had been the highlight of their tour in the United Kingdom.

As the form of the trials progresses from local through national to international level, the atmosphere changes; so too do the faces of the spectators. If you are visiting sheepdog trials for the first time, I strongly recommend that you start at the local ones as you can never really appreciate the apparent ease and skill of performances at international level until you have seen some of the less skilled, from both dog and handler.

The competitions at local trials can vary from those open to real novice dogs or handlers to the more experienced, and often include a special class for the lady competitors and, of course, the qualifying competitions for the national trials. Besides these there are classes for sheep-shearing, crook- or hurdle-making and many other attractions, all depending upon the ingenuity of the local committees or the suitable facilities of the venue. At times even a local gymkhana or ploughing match is run in conjunction with these events, and in some parts of the United Kingdom, particularly in Wales, there is a sheep section with classes for pens of local breeds, with cups and prizes for the best ram or ewe, and so on. These classes are of great interest to the farmers and are usually well filled. People may come from far afield to these trials. I once 'eavesdropped' on a couple of Australian sheep-farmers viewing the scene and discussing the various breed points with the judges at a pen of Welsh mountain sheep.

At the nationals the important issue at stake is the election of a team from the fifteen highest placed dogs to go forward to represent the country at the internationals. I know of many who plan their annual holiday to coincide with certain trials whenever they are held, and one couple told me they had not missed attending the English national since it was re-started after the war. In 1961 an Irish national was held in Northern Ireland and three competitors won their way to the team for the international for the first time. Then in 1965 Eire and the Isle of Man combined with Northern Ireland to become the Irish team and the fourth country to send a team consisting of four dogs, thus making a total of forty dogs to compete for the final honours at the international trials. Since 1976, as separate shepherd's classes have been discontinued, the number of dogs competing has been increased to fifteen of the highest-pointed dogs from England, Scotland and Wales, and five from Ireland, irrespective of whether the handlers are farmers or hired shepherds. The international trials have also been extended. Strong contingents of supporters from the Isle of Man as well as from Eire and Wales attend these trials to lend encouragement and have a short holiday. Each country in the UK in turn acts as host to these internationals. Supporters of the

106

national teams arrive in coachloads, the pedigree of every dog is known to them and the standard of performance they expect from them and the handlers is the main talking-point. If you happen to be staying in the same hotel as some of the Welsh supporters you can be assured of an amusing musical evening. The International Sheep Dog Society do a wonderful job in arranging accommodation, transport and entertainment for competitors or visitors and their families to these champion trials.

The Internationals, however, really live up to their name, both with the competitors and spectators, and a friendly holiday atmosphere abounds. The stand is full of rugged men leaning forward on their sticks, giving their own comments in hushed tones to the dogs on the field. I often speculate that if telepathy existed between these men and the dogs actually running, this could cause great confusion in the minds of the dogs. One may find oneself sitting next to an expert photographer from Japan with camera cocked ready for action; a shepherd from the Pyrenees, sporting a tam-o-shanter and plaid muffler, or a real live cowboy straight off 'the trail', and Welsh is not the only unfamiliar language to the ears.

The competitors or handlers are men whose expertise in the handling and training of sheepdogs is second to none. I have made many references to them elsewhere, and have little to add except to thank them for allowing us to appreciate their art. I make only one criticism and that is concerning the method of transport of their precious cargoes. One sees collies, sometimes as many as two or three, riding in the boot of the car, with sacking or a piece of cloth used as a wedge to allow in sufficient air. Admittedly, some of the boots are cunningly adapted, and we do not get many very hot days in this country, but even in our normal summer a car can become extremely hot if left standing in the sun even for a short time, or waiting in a queue to get into a show. This form of transport may be quite suitable for short journeys around the farm, when the dog may be too wet or muddy to go into the back of the car, but for a long journey, especially to a trial when the dog should appear groomed and clean anyway, I fail to understand the

logic. I have even seen dogs who have been expected to sleep overnight as well in these cramped conditions.

There is just as strong an element of competition and just as
many post-mortems afterwards on these trials grounds as in the
dog show world. Many keen competitors go to trials almost every
week, sometimes attending a three-day national and then another
local trial on the Sunday. For devotees, all forms of competition
with our dogs are infectious.

This brings us to the true purpose of these trials, the testing of
the working ability of the dogs. Each one is now a 'trial dog' who
may or may not be bred from trials-winning stock, but he is a
pedigree-registered sheepdog and probably a Border Collie. Equally
he may or may not be a good hill or pasture dog; that is of no consequence when he is running in a trial. What does matter is that he
has been trained for a definite task and his degree of ability in performing that task is being put to the test; so too is the degree of
sympathy or partnership that has been built up with his handler,
and in the final analysis luck will also play a part.

Of the fifty dogs that start out to compete for the coveted award
of Supreme Champion, only one can come through to win that
award, but many are the surprises and the hard luck tales on the
way. For quite unaccountable reasons things can go wrong and
even the sheep can fail to cooperate. During the Centenary Trials
at Bala, the day was almost unbearably hot, which was affecting
both the dogs and the sheep. One dog simply could not persuade
the sheep to go where he wanted them to; even frantic whistling
and re-directing from the handler failed to help, and in the end the
dog, who was still some way off, refused to obey any further orders
and stood facing his handler. Each time he was given a further
command he shook his head from side to side and finally he lay
down. Clearly he had had enough. The handler fully understood,
he recalled the dog and both retired to the tumultuous cheers of
the spectators.

Many people attending trials are struck by the behaviour of
these collies. Some are tied up to trees or fences, others to the
owners' cars; many roam about quite freely; yet there is rarely

any aggressiveness or fighting among them. Very occasionally a dog will pass another dog stiff-legged and hackles raised, but that is all. Most of the dogs are too busy watching their rivals, or just catching up on sleep.

On one of the days of the international trials a Brace and Driving Championship is held. These brace or doubles competitions where the handler is working two dogs, are always very popular with the spectators, and the concentration of the handler can almost be felt at the ringside. After the usual fetch and drive over the special course, when both dogs should be sharing the work equally, the flock is then shed and divided into two lots. One dog is required to pen his lot and then remain holding his charges or guarding them at the open pen. The other dog then wheels his charges into the second pen. Only a very well-trained and disciplined dog will remain at his post while his mate is working, within sight and sound of him, and it requires good holding powers to keep his charges from breaking out to try and join the rest of the flock. The course is completed when the handler is standing outside this second pen and both dogs are holding or guarding their respective pens. The dogs may either lie down or stand up, depending on their nature. This may sound a simple operation on paper, but only when one knows the ways of sheep and how cunning and determined they can be about sticking together, can one appreciate how well-trained a dog needs to be for this type of competition. Again, the skill and experience of these handlers in being able to direct two dogs with two different sets of whistles or commands, all apparently at the same time, never ceases to amaze me. Collies like to know the reason for obeying a given command and if they have been given this assurance they will have complete faith in the handler. Both on farms and on the trial ground the Border Collie is supreme at the singles and doubles work and in the driving contests they often excel over other types. To bring sheep up to the handler is almost a natural reaction in a dog, but to drive them away to no apparent destination the dog needs to have special confidence that his master knows what he is doing, and will give him further directions.

Great experience is also needed to select two dogs to work together as a team, as no two will have the same method of working, 'eye' or even temperament. Only someone who has actually seen an untrained or novice dog attempt to drive a flock of sheep can fully appreciate the apparent ease and skill with which these trials dogs operate, and this is particularly evident in the driving contests. I feel almost cheated as I have only once been able to watch the Driving Championships at the international trials; something has always occurred to prevent me, but I have seen some incredibly skilful driving displays in Australia.

At the end of this chapter will be found two I.S.D.S. sketch plans (Figs. 3a and 3b) of the courses for both the singles and doubles at national and international trials with details of the exercises or obstacles and the number of points allocated for each. Do not be misled as one overseas visitor was once, into thinking that each competitor will appear at the starting post dressed in plaid bonnet like the little symbol on the sketch. His dog, too, will be of a better type than the symbol, but personally I love this rather nostalgic note and hope the Society never see fit to have either modernized. Plans and courses vary in different localities.

In spite of a scale of points and definite guide-lines being laid down for judges, the task of the latter is a difficult and tiring one. No two judges could be expected to allocate the exact number of points in a given situation, it is according to how each judge sees the dog's movements. A further item which each judge will assess differently is the style in which each dog completes the whole run, not necessarily the fact that he has completed each section satisfactorily. From a spectator's point of view, noting the style of working of each dog is very interesting—the antics of the handlers are sometimes worth a study too.

Whatever your reason for attending a sheepdog trial you cannot fail to be entertained. It is often a long and tiring day for all concerned, sometimes starting at 7.30 in the morning and ending in the late afternoon, according to the number of entries and the standard of the work. I must stress once more that to get the maximum enjoyment from watching the real experts at work, you should first attend some local trials. If sheepdog trials were Olympic events I feel sure the United Kingdom could always be sure of a gold medal.

To conclude this chapter, I decided to use the following poem to describe a dog running in a trial. It may not meet with the approval of the Poet Laureate, but I think it is appropriate in the circumstances.

THE CHAMPION RUNS

A Borderer, black with snow-white patches,
    Bred in the hills round Walkerburn,
Confident winner in countless matches
    Stands at the post to wait his turn.

His ears are cocked and his eyes are steady
    Fixed on the bunch of distant sheep;
A word from his master finds him ready
    And sends him wide on his onward sweep.

Here is obedience stripped for duty
    Running with confidence side by side;
Here is intelligence crowned with beauty,
    Coupled with ardour, spurred by pride.

Onward and on like a flying shadow
    With watchful eyes where the wethers stand
He skims the brown of the winter meadow
    And closes in with his sheep in hand.

Some may rush in on their charge too keenly,
    Some may hustle those five too fast,
But the champion fathers them slow and cleanly
    Creeping in from a perfect cast.

Sheepdog Trials

Now with the planted poles appearing,
  Crouching, cautious, with instinct true
He moves them on with a careful steering,
  Steadies them, wheels them, guides them through.

Poles again, and new points for gaining—
  No more bringing but driving away;
Hardest test in a sheep-dog's training,
  Through them again! without delay.

Then to the hurdles' narrow gateway
  Slowly he brings them—ware and awake—
Stubborn sheep that ignore the straight way,
  Turn and challenge and try to break.

Patient he holds them; creeps, advances
  Paw after paw they face him—but
Watchful, on guard, he gives no chances;
  They turn, move in, and the gate is shut!

With scarcely so much as a whispered order,
  With hardly the hint of a lifted hand
So do the wonderful dogs of the Border
  Carry the pride of their lovely land.

                                      Will H. Ogilvie

(Written by Will H. Ogilvie about J. M. Wilson's 'Glen' when he
won the international in convincing style in 1946.)

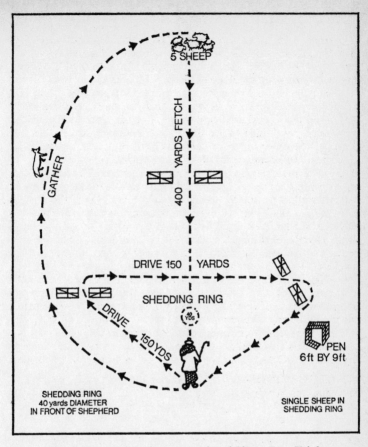

Fig. 3 Course plans for International Sheep Dog Trials

(a) Course for qualifying trials

(1) *COURSE*—The Course, Scale of Points and Time Limit now
fixed by the Directors are set out below and the responsibility for
laying out the Course in accordance with the Rules rests with the Trials
Committee and the Course Directors. (2) *Gathering 400 yards*—
In the outrun the dog may be directed on either side. A straight fetch
from the lift to the handler, through a centre gate (seven yards wide)
150 yards from the handler. No re-try at the gate is allowed. The
handler will remain at the post from the commencement of the outrun
and at the end of the fetch he will pass the sheep behind him.

(3) *Driving*—The handler will stand at the post and direct his dog to drive the sheep 450 yards over a triangular course through two sets of gates seven yards wide, a second attempt at either gate is NOT allowed. The drive ends when the sheep enter the shedding ring. The handler will remain at the post until the sheep are in the shedding ring. In the case of a short course, when the fetch is less than 400 yards, the drive will be lengthened when possible so that the total length of the fetch and drive is 850 yards, or as near to the length as is reasonably practicable. The drive may be either to left or right and shall be decided by the Trials Committee immediately prior to the Trial. (4) *Shedding*—Two unmarked sheep to be shed within a ring 40 yards in diameter. The dog must be in full control of the two sheep shed (in or outside the ring) otherwise the shed will not be deemed satisfactory. On completion of the shed the handler shall reunite his sheep before proceeding to pen. (5) *Penning*— The pen will be 6 feet by 9 feet with a gate 6 feet wide to which is secured a rope 6 feet long. On completion of shedding, the handler must proceed to the pen, leaving his dog to bring the sheep to the pen. The handler is forbidden to assist the dog to drive the sheep to the pen. The handler will close the gate. After releasing the sheep, the handler will close and fasten the gate. (6) *Single Sheep*—The handler will proceed to the shedding ring leaving the dog to bring the sheep from the pen to the ring. One of two marked sheep will be shed off within the ring and thereafter worn (in or outside the ring) to the judges' satisfaction. Handlers are forbidden to assist the dog in driving off, or attempting to drive off the single any distance or by forcing it on the dog.

SCALE OF POINTS—Outrun 20; Lifting 10; Fetching 20; Driving 20; Shedding 10; Penning 10; Single 10. Total 100. **TIME LIMIT**—15 minutes. No extension.

COURSE—(1)—*Gathering*—There will be 10 or such number of sheep as the Committee decide upon, in one lot in the centre of the field at a distance of approximately 800 yards. Both dogs will start at the same time. Crossing at the completion of the outrun is permissible but dogs should remain on the side to which they have crossed and they should not recross. The fetch should be straight through a gate (nine yards wide) in the centre of the field. Should the gate be missed no re-try is allowed. Each dog will keep its own side and the handler will remain at the post and at the end of the fetch will pass the sheep behind him. (2) *Driving*—The handler stands at the post and directs his two dogs to drive the sheep 600 yards over a triangular course through two sets of gates (nine yards wide), back to the handler. No re-try is allowed at either gate. Each dog is to keep to its own side and the handler must

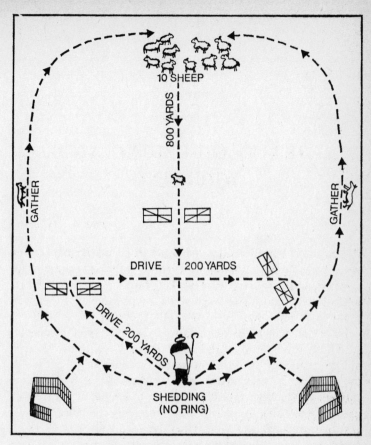

(b) Course for 'brace' championship

remain at the post until the end of the drive. The drive is finished when the sheep enter the shedding ring. (3) *Shedding*—The sheep will be divided into two equal lots by either dog inside the shedding ring; one lot will be driven off and left in charge of one dog—the other lot will be penned in a diamond shaped pen with an entrance of five feet and no gate. This dog will be left in charge while the other lot are penned by the other dog in a similar pen approximately 50 yards away.

SCALE OF POINTS—Gathering (Outrun 2 × 10: 20, Lifting 20 and Fetching 20) 60; Driving 20; Shedding 10; Penning (2 lots 10 plus 10) 20. Total 110. TIME LIMIT—25 minutes. No extension.

Chapter 4

HEALTH, BREEDING AND
WHELPING

Of the many considerations that have to be taken into account when breeding dogs, the most important is for what purpose the dog is required. In the case of working farm or sheepdogs, breeding is usually only undertaken when a replacement will soon be required or when there is a demand for the stock of a particularly good strain, and is therefore carried out by responsible people who have the interest of the breed at heart. There is, however, another category of breeders whom I consider to be totally irresponsible as they breed only for financial gain without a thought for quality or the eventual fate of the puppies. Pet shops are full of so-called Border Collies whose only claim to the title is that they are black and white. Dogs' homes are also full of similar types that have proved unsatisfactory pets. So often any puppy that is black, with four white feet and a white tip to its tail, is at once labelled a collie. It is essential that owners of true Border Collies as pets should think very carefully about what will be the fate of their litters before any breeding is undertaken, lest they too fall into the above category.

So we come back to the responsible breeder or one who knows what he wants to breed for, but who perhaps lacks the experience in this field. A really good stockman has a sort of built-in intuition with regard to putting the right animals together. He needs no written pedigree as it is all in his head; but this knowledge is born

116

of experience which is one of the few blessings that come with increasing years.

To improve one's stock should be the aim of every breeder. In the farming world all aspects of the working ability (or lack of it) in the parents should be studied before any programme is embarked upon, and great attention must be paid to the inheritance factor; this is where a properly understood pedigree can be of most use, except when one has been able to observe at first hand the character and performance of the progeny from either the dog or bitch one intends to breed from—bearing in mind that most breeders subscribe to the theory that 'like breeds like'. A study of the character and performance of the stock from any chosen pedigree will definitely make breeding for improvement a much less hit-and-miss affair. Even with the best planned mating you will be lucky if you get more than one or two pups from litters which inherit the qualities you had expected, but the sale of surplus pups from litters such as these can help with the cost of rearing even if it does not fully compensate for the loss of work from the bitch for the few weeks before and after whelping.

Many of these surplus pups will go to pet homes, so temperament is another important factor in a breeding programme, and one to which I give top priority myself. Good or bad temperament is not always hereditary as it can quite often be influenced by early upbringing and environment as I have explained elsewhere. A dog or bitch that does not have the correct temperament is difficult if not impossible to train for work, and also makes an unreliable companion or pet.

This brings me to the question of the good and bad points that stock can inherit from their parents. However good a performer a dog may be, either on the farm or trials ground, it does not reach its full potential unless it can also transmit these good qualities to its progeny. If both parents have one or two similar good points, such as excelling in 'eye', good driving or gathering ability, great patience or stamina and so on, then it is safe to assume that most of their progeny will inherit these good points. In my experience it has never been a satisfactory operation to try to counteract a bad fault in one parent by putting it to a mate that excels in the desired direction. I have found that one only doubles up on some other fault. I prefer to try to stamp in the good points and learn to live with the others, or attempt to overcome them by careful and studied training and selection.

It is here too that good stockmen and knowledgeable breeders take full advantage of their experience when planning their litters, and it is to this category of breeder that one should apply when seeking a pup. These breeders can supply details of the family history plus any particular characteristics the pup may be likely to inherit, then the purchaser can make up his mind if this is the strain he is requiring either for work or as a pet. No doubt pet shops and backyard breeders fulfil some definite function, but I am of the opinion that unless the breeder can pass on to the purchaser full details of ancestry, date of birth, date of worming, diet sheet and information on the general care of the pup, then they do not have sufficient experience to call themselves 'breeders' in the accepted term. Only people with great experience in collies should purchase from casual breeders when they are sure they know their own requirements; but someone purchasing a collie for the first time should always approach a recognized breeder. The International Sheep Dog Society, the Kennel Club, or any local canine club can usually supply names of good breeders in your district.

It may seem unnecessary to say that breeding stock should always be kept in top condition, but many breeders fail in this respect and keep both sires and dams on only a subsistence diet, and resulting litters get off to a poor start in life. Parasites, especially on dogs and bitches working with stock, cause a lowering of condition almost as much as does a poor diet. Overwork, or no proper sleeping quarters, are also contributory factors to lack of condition. A dog that has to use up all its food energy in keeping warm while chained to an old barrel in the open after a long working day, and with only a few lumps of tripe for a meal, cannot keep in top breeding condition, and if bred from at all the drain and strain will shorten its life and produce weak stock.

There is also the question of breeding to type if we are to keep the Border Collie as a pure breed. As I mentioned earlier, as far back as 1850 a pure strain or recognized type of sheepdog was being bred which we have since come to regard as a Border Collie, and up to a few years ago this strain was being bred from by responsible people who jealously guarded this aspect. Today we have too many irresponsible breeders who do not care about type. Many people say it is only working ability that counts, but I maintain that a collie has got to be the right type, made on the right lines to give the top performance, and there are many good breeding strains or lines to choose from. Study the top winning dogs at national or international level and note the uniformity of type, and then study the lines of descent. Those not built on the right lines with the correct temperament fall on the way to the top, but all the top winners will come from certain good strains.

I sometimes wonder if the growing popularity of the Border Collie for obedience work has been in the best interests of breeding to type. One has only to observe the varied types seen in the obedience ring that are registered as Border Collies. The owners of these collies are among those who subscribe to the 'ability not looks' theory, but if some effort is not made by these owners to standardize the type as well as the consistency in performance, in a very short time the breed will be so diversified in type that it will not be possible to recognize these dogs as Border Collies, and we will be back to the pre-1800 era; this is one of the reasons why I feel it is so important to have the official Breed Standard laid down as guide lines to breed to, and these observations also apply to temperament.

In dog breeding one can only reproduce the qualities that are already in the parents, and however carefully you try to avoid or reproduce a given quality the end result is still a matter of luck, and determined by the dominant genes in either parent. One reads a great deal about homozygous or heterozygous individuals, also dominant and recessive traits, and I have listened to breeders discussing these factors at great length when planning the mating of their bitches, but I have yet to meet anyone whose breeding stock has produced the perfect litter from such studies. I continue to be a firm believer in intuition, which of course includes consideration of all these factors, but not in a rigid or academic way.

However, it is downright foolish and irresponsible to breed from stock that is known to have any hereditary defects such as hip-dysplasia, slipping stifles or any eye defects. These can in any case occur in stock born of parents who are themselves quite free of them. If this is the case why not simply continue to breed with animals known to have these defects, especially if they are good workers or trials winners? But it is just because breeders have been careless regarding these aspects in the past that they occur at all in today's collies. We simply must make a firm stand from the outset if we are to get working stock as clear as possible of any hereditary defects that undoubtedly interfere with their work. It may take several generations, but the International Sheep Dog Society has made a good start with the introduction of testing of collies for progressive retinal atrophy. I give a brief description of these defects and their consequences later in this chapter.

I am a firm believer in having pet dogs neutered, and if vets could convert more owners to this way of thinking there would be no need for the mass destruction of dogs that has to take place each year. Ask any vet and he will tell you what the dog has never experienced he or she cannot miss. The same pet owners who decry this idea regarding dogs are often the very ones who think it is quite in order to have their pet cat 'done' almost before it is old enough. In my own experience the only drawback I have encountered with neutered dogs or bitches is the need for a careful watch on their diet, especially as they get older, when they tend to put on weight. If you do consider such a step with regard to your pet, make sure, if it is a bitch, that she is not spayed until after her first season, and it goes without saying that a dog should be fully entire before he can be castrated, although vasectomy is now becoming more popular and has some advantages. Bitches can also be spayed after they have had a litter; many bitches that have never had a litter need a hysterectomy in later life because of some

120

womb disorder—and much pain and distress could have been avoided if they had been spayed in their youth. If you do take this step, get a dated certificate from your vet as proof.

It will be appreciated from the points I have made in this chapter that dog breeding carries with it many responsibilities if we are to keep both the mental and physical qualities for which the Border Collie is world famous. If you are contemplating breeding for the first time then I beg you to become a responsible breeder, giving due consideration to the reputation of the breed which in turn will benefit you. It is always better to be proud of your stock; if you are likely to be ashamed of it then you had better have it put down before you spend money on rearing puppies. Make sure too that you as an owner are worthy of your dogs—they never stint on their repayments to you.

Before I conclude this section, there is one question we have left unanswered—price. I feel strongly that reputable breeders deserve good prices for their stock since the sale is backed by years of experience which they can and do pass on to the purchaser. It is foolish of the public to pay high prices for a pup from a pet shop or other source when no background or guarantee of quality can be given. These premises fulfil a need in relieving pet owners of surplus puppies but I question if these puppies should have been born in the first place. Purchasers should never be in a hurry to buy a pup. Take time and great care in choosing from the right source and background, remembering that it will be a member of the family for many years.

Experienced breeders need not trouble to read the following pages except for general interest, to compare my methods with their own. The information is intended for those about to breed a litter of Border Collies for the first time and who are dedicated to the improvement of the breed. The advice is based on my own personal experience over some thirty years of breeding and training collies of all varieties.

GENERAL HEALTH

Under this heading I propose to give a layman's description of some of the health hazards that usually are peculiar to collies. Before we go on to consider general health problems, it is worth noting that a dog which mixes with other dogs and gets around a fair amount, builds up a reasonable resistance to disease in the same way as does a child who is brought up in the company of other children rather than in a clinical environment, but of course it can also be a carrier of disease. So the responsible thing to do is to have one's dog immunized. If it is not, and simply kept away from other dogs, it is far more likely to pick up any disease with which it comes into contact at any time. This particularly applies to sheepdogs working on the hills or isolated farms and also to house pets in remote areas. There are two schools of thought on this subject; those who do not believe in it and never have their dogs inoculated, and those who do. Anyone whose dogs have ever suffered or died due to contracting one of the diseases which can be prevented by immunization can rest assured that they would quickly come round to the latter school of thought. Dogs can also be 'carriers' without showing signs of the disease themselves, so it is very selfish as well as unwise not to have all the puppies immunized at the proper age. These inoculations or vaccinations (the term used depends on the type of vaccine used and how it works on the system) are referred to as 'shots' in many countries outside the United Kingdom. I think this term is very appropriate and avoids confusion. A dog can sometimes develop one of these diseases in spite of immunization, but the effects are usually slight. To prevent this happening it is a wise precaution to arrange for booster doses once a year; two of these are usually considered sufficient to cover a dog for life, but it depends upon the type used. The choice of the type of vaccine must be left to the discretion of the vet as he will then administer the latest tested one on the market. Certain vaccines must not be given to dogs intended for export as the effect will remain in the bloodstream for some time, in

122

which case when a dog is blood-tested by the health authorities of the importing country it will not pass the quarantine regulations.

Most owners arrange for routine inoculation of their pups and this is usually done at twelve and fourteen weeks old, by which time the pup is very often in the care of its new owner. For breeders who are likely to be at risk owing to their circumstances, it is possible to use an eight-week-old and twelve-week-old inoculation cycle, but this is not routine for the average pet owner. At twelve weeks the immunity which the pup has received from its dam is at its lowest ebb, and this coincides with the time at which the vaccination of the pup will create the maximum immunological response in its body. The average pup will receive shots of a combined vaccine which cover the four major diseases suffered by the dog. As with many vaccines the immunological response to canine distemper is good and few dogs need more than two inoculations during their lifetime; but on the other hand the response to the leptospiral infections is very weak, hence it is important to remember that any immunity (i.e. antibodies in the body) can be overwhelmed if the infective dose (i.e. invading antigens) is high enough.

The four main diseases which can be prevented by these 'shots' are as follows. Firstly, the one we are all familiar with and which is not such a frequent occurence these days due to these precautions. This is:

Distemper with its more virulent form—*Hard pad*.
Canine distemper. Symptoms:
1. Persistent high temperature.
2. Gastro-enteritis.
3. Cough, and other signs of respiratory distress.
4. Ocular-nasal pustular discharge after a period of time, usually one to two weeks.
5. Skin involvement with pustules, loss of hair and keratinisation (hard pad).
6. Involvement of the central nervous system with fits and convulsions.

The insidious onset of this disease is followed by a deceptively progressive illness which is usually fatal, with death in convulsions. Recovery is a possibility but the dog is often physically and mentally weak for the rest of its life; it usually shows some kind of nervous disability and may even have periodic fits. Treatment is in general symptomatic rather than specific. Expensive antiserum is available, but its use is questionable once the condition has become established, so preventive inoculation is greatly to be preferred to any attempt to treat the disease.

Secondly, *canine* or *viral hepatitis* which affects the liver. A dog can suffer from it for some time without it being diagnosed and can be ill for quite a time before the disease eventually manifests itself. Meantime a dog can spread it in various ways as it is highly contagious. The symptoms are those usually seen when there is disease of the liver, namely, gastro-enteritis with thirst, pyrexia and, ultimately, jaundice. It is a condition to be given particular consideration by breeders as it is often the cause of the deaths of whole litters of puppies in the first weeks of their life. Corneal opacity, or 'blue eyes' caused by oedema of the cornea, in conjunction with these other symptoms, is practically specific of the disease. The mediocre response to inoculation means that many adult dogs can easily contract the disease, and often the mild symptoms ensuing are ignored, but the dog is rendered a dangerous carrier. Entire families of puppies can be wiped out, the nature of the condition being discovered by laboratory examination of specimens submitted from the post mortem following the pups' sudden death. Treatment with antibiotics is of minimal value and the best response is to injections of antiserum if they are started early enough. However, the volume of antiserum that has to be injected is relatively large and the administration of it can be extremely distressing to all parties.

Thirdly, *Leptospira canicola* is a disease which affects the kidneys and the liver, and is often fatal unless discovered and treated before too much damage has occurred, but even if a good recovery is made a dog needs to be kept on a very careful diet for the rest of its life.

Fourthly, *Leptospira icterohaemorrhagiae* which many farm

dogs contract as it is carried by rats. This is often not apparent until it has reached the jaundice stage, and in the meantime it can be passed on to humans.

Leptospiral nephritis and *Hepatitis* are bacterial induced diseases best considered in conjunction with the above as the symptoms produced by *Leptospira canicola* and *Leptospira icterohaemorrhagiae* are very similar. The antibody response to inoculation is very weak and annual boosters are recommended. The cases are usually presented to the veterinary surgeon as dogs running a temperature with vomiting and diarrhoea, thirst and often interior abdominal pain. Ultimately cases where the liver is the principal organ involved will show jaundice. Analysis of the urine will reveal if the liver or kidneys are primarily involved, or if both organs are diseased. Mortality of untreated dogs is high. A relatively long course of antibiotic treatment, often combined with saline infusions in severe cases, generally produces a satisfactory cure. However, it is necessary to point out that the diseased organs are permanently damaged, and the owner of such a recovered dog must be constantly aware of the specific diet it will require and of the fact that its physical condition will often be poor. Also, an absolute cure is difficult to achieve and stress to such a dog for whatever other reason will often precipitate a further crisis. The main point to realize is that inoculation is infinitely preferable to treatment, i.e. prevention is better than cure.

When purchasing a puppy ascertain if it has had any of its 'shots' and if so be sure to get the vet's certificate which states when they were given and for which diseases and when the booster doses are due. If the puppy has not yet been treated, take it to the vet as soon as possible, or seek his advice as to the correct age to have the 'shots' done and so on. This will allow the vet time to order the correct vaccine; you will appreciate that it is not possible for him to keep a stock of every type of drug or vaccine always available.

Fleas, Lice and Other Pests or Parasites

These are all injurious to health. They cause skin troubles, loss of condition, and may carry tape-worm eggs. It should be routine practice to dust your dogs and their beds with a recommended insect powder once a week in summer, less often in winter. Aerosol sprays and insecticidal shampoos can also be used for the prevention of infestation. I am not at all in favour of flea collars, much advertised as they are, particularly where breeding stock is concerned. There is no doubt that these are very efficient, but like so many of today's 'cure-alls', we cannot always predict any possible side effects. I have known many dogs and bitches who have developed an allergy to the substances on these collars after having prolonged contact with the skin. These have taken the form of skin disorders and created breeding problems, where none have occurred before. There is no definite proof that these collars have caused the disorders, but it is significant that when they were removed, order was restored within a short time. Rather than take risks I prefer to stick to the old-fashioned method of trying to keep the dog, the bedding and the grooming kits as clean as possible, and using a tried and tested insecticide when necessary.

Ticks

These can be problematic in this country, but still more so to dog owners in many other parts of the world. There are several brands of special shampoo that are very effective for killing the ticks and which will prevent them from settling on the skin if applied strictly according to the directions. Never pull out a tick unless you see that its head is not buried in the dog's skin. If you leave the head in, it sometimes causes a nasty poisonous sore. Paraffin or a lighted cigarette end applied to the tick used to be considered very effective, but both can be dangerous. So too can puncturing with a needle or pin.

Worms

In this country roundworms and tapeworms are the dog's most

common enemies, but abroad there are many other types of worm which have to be remedied. All puppies have roundworms and as the puppy grows so do the worms. Personally I dislike wasting good food on worms so I dose the puppies as early as possible. I have too often seen this left until too late, and I refer again to worming in the section on rearing puppies.

Tapeworms

The presence of this worm in the dog usually manifests itself by the appearance of particles like dried rice left on the coat or skin around the anus, but prior to this the dog will be noticeably out of condition and listless and have a staring dry coat. For the surest diagnosis, send a sample of the excreta to a vet for examination, and if it proves positive then the vet will prescribe the right dose. The dog's correct weight should also be supplied. Incorrect or excessive dosing of a dog for a tapeworm can be very dangerous.

Collie Nose

This is a condition akin to herpes or a cold sore in a human. It is an allergy caused by a reaction of the skin to sunlight. Fortunately it only affects a very few collies and although it looks unpleasant it has no serious consequences, but is of an hereditary nature.

Heatstroke

Collies are particularly prone to this, and prevention is in the hands of the owner; but should it occur it takes the form of a mild fit, with the dog lying stretched out as if dead. Keep him in the shade, bathe his head with cold water or keep it covered with a wet towel, making sure he can breathe properly. Keep him very quiet for some considerable time even after full recovery. In extreme cases in hot climates, when he has been overcome while at work, I have seen a dog immersed in a river.

Anal Glands

Many collies suffer from the glands inside the anus becoming infected and/or impacted. The dogs can be seen licking themselves a lot and they often walk in rather a peculiar way. A dog can sometimes be seen dragging its bottom along the ground, or sledging. This is often taken as a sign of worms when in fact the dog is suffering from anal gland trouble. If the dog is having a lot of pain or irritation he will not eat, since he knows that some of what goes in must come out and it is this process that is causing him discomfort. A vet will quickly squeeze out the anal glands and if they are very infected he will also give a shot of penicillin to help clear up the infection quickly. Once a dog has a tendency to this complaint it may recur quite often, and needs to be watched.

Collie Eye Anomaly (C.E.A.)

This is an hereditary eye defect where the degree that exists at birth remains constant during the dog's life. So many show collies in the United States were found to be affected by this that compulsory testing was introduced. Fortunately Dr Keith Barnett, the great authority on dog's eye diseases, and well-known in sheepdog circles, assures me that the incidence of this disease in the Border Collies which he has examined in the United Kingdom is almost negligible, but it is worth mentioning since it is exclusive to our shepherding breeds.

Progressive Retinal Atrophy (P.R.A.)

This is a much more serious hereditary eye disease which affects many breeds, and it is particularly tragic when it affects a working collie. Unlike C.E.A., P.R.A., as its name implies, is progressive; dogs affected get steadily worse until totally blind. (Mercifully both diseases are painless.) It is very sad, and such a waste, to hear of a really good collie affected by P.R.A., as one knows that sooner or later his career must end prematurely due to this condition. Sometimes demonstrations are given by farmers at local or agricultural shows where a blind collie is used. This is of course a remarkable feat, and the performance can be popular with the audience. For me it is a sad one that I would rather not witness. It must be appreciated that it can only be undertaken by handlers with a very high degree of skill with dogs and knowledge of the ways of sheep. The dogs themselves will also have reached a very high degree of training, for their performance on these occasions will be literally a matter of 'blind obedience'.

If a dog has gone blind slowly over a period, as with P.R.A., the effect upon his daily life is slight as his wonderful scenting powers and the radar system in his whiskers will help him overcome his disability. We have a totally blind and deaf collie at home at present. She goes for regular walks with us and finds her way around with no difficulty even in the woods, but only because she is familiar with her surroundings. To take her to strange places without a lead would be sheer cruelty.

To prevent P.R.A. from spreading, the International Sheep Dog Society introduced facilities for eye testing at many of their sheepdog trials. Dr Barnett now regularly attends these meetings and tests any collies presented to him, giving a certificate if the dog is found clear. A Border Collie is declared permanently clear when it is over two years old, as P.R.A. can develop at any time up to this age. With the rough and smooth show collies the age is three years for a permanent certificate under the BVA/KC scheme, but if the collie is tested and found clear at an earlier age, its owner is issued with an interim certificate and the dog should be presented again for a further test at or after three years old. If this disease is to be wiped out, which may take several generations, it is absolutely vital that affected dogs should not be bred from. The International Sheep Dog Society will only accept for registration puppies of registered parents carrying a clear P.R.A. certificate, except at double fees. As yet we do not know what will be the requirement of the Kennel Club on this matter with regard to Border Collies.

I must stress again that these brief descriptions are only to give

E   129

the novice owner some idea of the diseases most likely to affect collies, but I think it would be imprudent not to mention the most dreaded disease of all, as follows.

Rabies

This affects not only dogs, but also cats, cattle, deer, mice, voles and foxes—in fact every mammal. It will be seen then that the farming community is particularly vulnerable, with sheepdogs and gundogs at greatest risk. In humans the disease is known as hydrophobia (an acute fear of water) and is contracted through the saliva from the bite of an infected animal. A bite from an infected cat is considered to be the most dangerous. We have the powers in our own hands, both geographically and by law, to prevent this disease from invading our shores, and it is the duty of all of us to uphold the laws. Here as in all other matters dealing with health, prevention is better than cure.

Naturally Border Collies are also subject to any of the other canine diseases, but on the whole, they are very tough and healthy, being descended on the 'survival of the fittest' principle through so many generations. It is the responsibility of present-day breeders to see that it remains that way. The services of a good vet are invaluable and money for veterinary bills is always well spent, but the privilege of visiting a vet or having him come to your premises should be discretionary, apart from the cash consideration. Many years ago I was waiting in my vet's surgery one evening when an urgent telephone call came through for a vet to visit a client as soon as possible. The vet on duty came out and enquired of the other two people and myself waiting in the surgery if our visits were of an urgent nature, and if not, would we mind returning next day; he felt he should leave at once to attend to this call as he was the vet in the practice nearest to the residence. He explained that when this particular person requested a vet to visit her as soon as possible, the matter was really urgent and you dropped everything and went. Now I happened to know the lady in question and had the highest regard for her myself. She was a very experienced breeder, an ex-hospital staff-nurse and a most knowledgeable, level-headed person. I have never forgotten that incident and hoped that over the years my own reputation with this vet would be held in such high regard.

When you know your own dog really well you can tell at once if he is ill or off colour. This may just be some temporary upset or the dog may be sickening for something more serious. The surest way to find out is by taking his temperature. A dog's normal temperature is 101°F; any significant rise or lowering of temperature should be viewed with caution, except when a bitch is whelping. If the temperature is normal then unless the dog's condition gets considerably worse there is no need to panic, but take the temperature again several hours later; then, if it is up, send for a vet. To take a dog's temperature, insert the thermometer into the rectum, having first wetted or oiled it and made sure that the mercury is fully shaken down. The idea of taking a collie's temperature may seem absurd to some owners and I confess that at one time I thought the idea rather far-fetched. However, once you realize that the temperature of an apparently sick dog is normal, you can be fairly certain it is something you can deal with yourself, and it relieves you of a lot of worry.

GENERAL CARE AND GROOMING

Attention to these two subjects can help greatly to keep any dog in good health but they are often sadly neglected. Ideally a working dog should be examined and groomed every day in the same way as a working hunter or a racehorse. However, even a weekly inspection and grooming is better than none. It is surprising how quickly this routine can become a good habit and time can be found to carry it out. By examination I mean having a look at the teeth and inside the mouth; if the dog is off his food or bad-tempered, this may be caused by his having a broken tooth or an ulcer.

Nose and Eyes

Both should be checked, and if either are sore or discharging a remedy can be applied before it becomes a major problem. Ears should be cleaned out frequently with a clean cloth, and inspected for signs of canker or, as often happens in a working collie, a grass seed which may have got lodged in the ear, causing a lot of pain.

Feet

Good sound feet are very important to a working collie. Examine in between the toes and the pads, paying particular attention to the 'stopper' pad which is situated behind and just above the dew claw. A collie having to stop suddenly while moving at great speed will be seen to throw his toes upwards in the last few strides and use this pad as extra braking power—hence the name. Collies when 'driving' on hard surfaces or stubble can easily rip these pads, causing a great deal of pain and, sometimes, lameness. In the days when sheep and cattle were driven along the flint roads to market it was quite usual to see the dogs that accompanied them return home with their feet raw and bleeding. Collies working on grass need their nails cut quite frequently to avoid lameness. Those working on harder surfaces hardly ever need this attention.

Coat

One of the special attractions of a collie is the lack of the usual strong 'doggy' smell associated with many other breeds. This attribute can only be maintained if the dog is kept clean and groomed. There is nothing more depressing than to see a dejected, dirty collie with lumps of dead fur handing from its coat and looking for all the world like one of the sheep it has rounded up after wintering out. To see them in this condition in front of the public at trials is an insult. All that is needed is a good pony dandy brush, a comb, plus your own time. The more often the grooming is done, the less time it takes.

Pests or any skin troubles will be discovered when the dog is groomed. As I have said, he should ideally be groomed for even a few minutes each day as this stimulates his whole system and tones him up. It is not just a cosmetic operation to make him look pretty; it helps the circulation, and by removing the dead hairs in the coat together with loose dirt it helps the lubrication of the skin and nourishes the coat.

I have either bought or rescued the most miserable, half-starved moth-eaten looking collies from farms where they have been neglected, and within a month, with correct food, a little fussing and good grooming these dogs would not have been recognized by their former owners. Needless to say I never took a dog that did not have a good temperament as I wanted to be sure of finding them good homes later on.

Retirement in Old Age

To us humans this is a stage in one's life that we either look forward to or dread, but our dogs bear old age with greater dignity. Among farmers and flockmasters the necessity to replace a dog that is no longer pulling its weight is as essential as having to replace a machine. Economics dictate that it is foolish to keep a worn-out machine, and however sad the farmer may feel at the loss of a faithful friend, a quick despatch to a happier place is essential. This in my opinion is the correct decision, if one has the courage to carry it out. It is very doubtful if a retired dog, used to working, is ever really happy just wandering around the farm. He needs human companionship, a softer life and much more care in his retirement than his owner would be able to give him. Sometimes the right pet homes can be found, but readjustment does not come easily to an older dog, and few people are prepared to take on the responsibility of caring for a dog past its prime; many sheepdogs are really only happy when working.

With a pet collie the case is quite different: we can allow all the sentiment we wish so long as the dog is not suffering in any way. Healthy collies usually live to a good age if fed and treated properly. Feeding an old dog is very important. Food should be of the best quality but reduced in quantity, two small meals being preferable to one large one. Moderation in all things is the motto here. Routine examination of the dog is advisable and good regular grooming is essential. Grooming an older dog acts almost as a tonic, stimulating the sluggish blood circulation which in turn helps other parts of the body. The old coat is not fully cast with the seasons in the older dog, but tends to be shed almost all the time; so regular grooming assists this new growth, to say nothing of saving the housewife the trouble of having to remove hairs from the carpet.

Decaying teeth can cause bad breath and pain, and if teeth are kept regularly scaled much of this decay can be prevented. Do not let the dog lie by a fire and then take him for his last walk at night in the pouring rain and put him to bed wet. Dry him off first to avoid rheumatism. Regular exercise is important, but the amount must be adjusted to his physical condition. Old dogs tend to get lazy, but if they are sound in heart, wind and limb, they should be exercised, even on a lead if necessary.

The advice given in the following chapters is based on my own experience and is intended purely as a guide-line in a particular situation. Only a qualified vet can give authoritative advice as he will know the circumstances both within the home and on that particular farm, in the same way as the general practitioner looks after the families in his care.

HOUSING

Conditions under which some dogs live can range from the sublime comfort of father's armchair to a broken old barrel in a sea of mud. I have seen first-class working collies, literally the farmer's third arm, kept in housing conditions far inferior to those of his pigs or hens. I have seen these dogs coming into the farmyard dripping wet, covered with mud, tired and hungry, and the farmer will at once chain them up and go off for a cup of tea or to see his other stock—without, quite often, even checking if the dog has a drink of fresh water. If a bowl or bucket has been provided near his chain it has usually been turned over during the day by some other farm stock. When the farmer's own prize bull, his hunter or his children's pony comes into the yard in the same condition I have witnessed the V.I.P. treatment they receive before being bedded down for the night. Surely it is not too much to ask of any owner of a dog that has given so much of himself, helping all day, to see that he is provided with dry, comfortable and draught-proof sleeping quarters in which to rest?

When one comes across a bad-tempered or very nervous collie, and makes further enquiries into its background, in almost all cases that dog has either been brought up on a chain or confined to a small space for long periods without human company. I am not opposed to dogs being kept temporarily on chains when it is necessary, but not as a living condition. A collie is well equipped to stand the cold and the wet if it is able to move around and shake itself, as when running at work; but to be forced to lie in a wet bed, unable to move around very far to keep warm, is unreasonable, heartless and wasteful treatment. Dogs kept under these conditions are usually crippled with rheumatism by the time they reach four to five years old.

An old barrel (now very difficult to obtain) may be adequate kennelling for a dog, with two important qualifications. Firstly, it should have a floor laid inside to prevent damp rising, so that the dog can lie down on a flat surface and is not always forced to lie with his back in a curve. To get maximum rest a dog must be able to lie flat out; if he cannot, he will lie outside the kennel. Secondly, the barrel should be inside some form of barn, shed or stable where the area around it is dry, but I question whether this basic type of accommodation is reasonable in these affluent days. Few owners are so poor that they cannot provide something better. If an ordinary type of kennel is provided these two qualifications also apply.

It is doubtful if those responsible for keeping their collies in the bad conditions I have described will ever read this book, or if they do they are unlikely to change their methods for the better care and comfort of the best unpaid skilled worker they are ever likely to employ; but in fairness to these dogs it is a problem that warrants mention. Perhaps when checks are made by inspectors to ascertain if owners are complying with the new Acts, this might prick the conscience of some of these careless people. If it does, and owners keeping collies under sub-standard conditions can be persuaded to provide better accommodation, then these laws will at least have had some success.

Ideally each dog should have its own suitable kennel and run, and the bed off the ground to prevent draughts. There is a large range of suitable kennelling on the market and the choice must remain a personal matter depending upon location and pocket. For dog beds the new fibreglass types are the best possible investment. They are almost indestructible, very light, hygienic and easy to clean. They cannot harbour any pests and can be cleaned with the wipe of a rag; the cost is almost the same as a wooden bed. Of course if you are a handyman you can probably knock up a good kennel and bed very inexpensively, but wood does have some drawbacks. For flooring in home-made wooden beds, you cannot beat chipboard given several coats of a sealing compound.

There is a wide range of suitable bedding material. On farms this is usually straw, which should be changed very frequently as it becomes either dusty or damp very quickly, depending on the weather. However, many collies dislike any kind of bedding, preferring to sleep on the bare boards. If this is the case, make sure the board is kept clean and dry. By far the best, cheapest and most hygienic and absorbent material for bedding is newspaper. If the dog still prefers the bare boards, at least providing newspaper in the bed helps to keep it clean and dry. What is more, the dog is doing this job himself while he is scrapping it up and pushing it to one side, and if eaten it is quite safe. Wood wool used to be considered the best bedding material, but the price is now quite prohibitive. I dislike sawdust in kennels for any purpose. Wood shavings are excellent, but again too costly for most of us.

So long as you have a good bed then the floor of the kennel and run can be of concrete or cement, which is easy to keep clean, but again it is advisable to apply several coats of a sealing compound as this prevents rising damp and facilitates the drying process when you wash it out.

When a dog comes in from work, if he is wet and muddy he should be rubbed down with straw, a towel or even with sacking (a fast-disappearing commodity); then he should be examined for any injuries, thorns or brambles caught in his coat. In the old days one could rub a dog down with a chamois leather which dried a coat in no time, but this is an expensive luxury these days. However, a big Wettex cloth is equally absorbent, if not so long-lasting. Feet should be examined for cuts or thorns—all this need only take a few minutes and the discovery of anything amiss, if dealt with as soon as possible, may prevent the dog from being off work the following day. Only after this short inspection should the dog be put to bed. I wonder how many farmers or flockmasters faithfully carry out such a routine? True shepherds, who know the worth of their dogs, and many other owners I know of, do take great care of their collies. I only wish there were many more such people.

As I have mentioned before, these points regarding the well-being of a Border Collie are intended for those new to these dogs; most books on general dog care can never cover the complexities of the situations that surround all aspects of this breed. If I were writing about show collies it would be only too easy to cover the subject of housing or kennelling in this one chapter, but with the Border Collies one has at all times to bear in mind what purpose the dog is fulfilling, and then try to recommend a suitable solution for the occasion or conditions existing on the farm. For instance, at the beginning of this section I briefly alluded to the family pet in father's armchair, but even the pet collie needs a bed to itself and in particular a place in the house it can consider its very own; and by being there he cannot be accused of being in anyone's way. Then we must consider the collie that is partly a house dog but kept for some form of work—he is usually kennelled outside. The same rules apply regarding dry, draught-proof bedding and adequate space to move around both inside and in any outside run.

Collies are great jumpers and if they can't stand back and get a good take-off to get over an obstacle they will scramble over it. If it is not possible to have the wire in your run sufficiently high—at least six feet—then one can either cover the run with wire mesh or garden netlon stretched over wires, or put an extra strand or two of wire on right angle supports leaning inwards along the top. This has had the effect of stopping the dog when he almost reaches the top as his head touches the overhanging wire. I have always had to take these precautions when the Border Collies are put into my kennel runs.

Collies get bored quickly, so never leave them too long without attention, especially young puppies, and never leave excreta lying around in the kennels or runs. Collies are a particularly clean breed and the bitches pay a lot of attention to keeping the puppies clean and clearing up any messes they make, even after they have been weaned. The pups watch her doing this and think they should do the same. This can be habit-forming and is most undesirable. There are of course other reasons for puppies eating excreta, but this is the main one; keeping the run clean will prevent this habit before it begins.

Clean water should always be available for dogs or puppies and preferably in a container that cannot be overturned. On a farm an old pig-trough or an automatic drinking bowl from the cowshed, screwed to the wall (minus the automatic device) is ideal, even if a little difficult to empty and keep clean; otherwise use a good heavy galvanized bowl if available. Once dogs or puppies get the habit of upsetting the water bowls or having a game of paddling they cause an awful nuisance. I do not recommend pottery drinking bowls for outside use; they are too easily broken, causing cut lips or feet if the dogs play with the broken parts, and in winter the ice causes the bowls to break.

FEEDING

My mother used to quote the saying that a collie could live on the smell of an oily rag, and indeed in the past many wretched collies lived and worked on very frugal diets. It was a struggle for a small farmer or a shepherd to keep his family, let alone his dogs, on the agricultural wages he received. The family diet consisted mainly of bread and potatoes, while that of the dog was porridge and scraps, both occasionally being supplemented with a rabbit or some pork. Collies earned the reputation of sly thieves, along with other accusations levelled against them—often true, but it is little wonder their behaviour was not all it should have been when you consider the treatment they received. Flockmasters and drovers could usually afford to feed their dogs a little better and indeed found this necessary in order to maintain the hard physical condition the dogs needed to do the work required of them. Boiled barley or oatmeal with some milk or gravy was the dog's staple diet long ago. Meat was never given as it was felt that if once they acquired the taste for it they might be tempted to kill the sheep or lambs; many old-fashioned farmers still subscribe to this theory today. However, it is a fact that properly fed dogs are much less likely to hunt for food or have the desire to kill unless hunting in packs. Since man has replaced the pack leader, dogs will follow his example of discipline and they look to him to provide their meals.

In the wild state a dog lives mainly on meat, thus deriving all the nourishment by devouring the whole carcase. If a dog kills a rabbit or a hare it will at once open up the stomach and from the herbage contents will obtain most of his mineral requirements and the rest from the flesh, bones and fur. It is believed that the fur passing through the bowels collects up and dispels any worms. I have never proved this belief but I do know that old-time shepherds and gamekeepers actually gave fur and feathers to their dogs regularly for this purpose. This was before the days of worm tablets. The digestive juices in a dog are capable of coping with even the raw bones when well crunched up, but if bones are cooked they cannot be acted upon by the digestive juices and then become a danger when eaten, apart from the risk of splinters.

Although meat is a dog's natural food, it is not absolutely

essential to his diet providing substitutes such as fish, eggs and milk are plentiful; but to maintain a dog in good physical condition for work he must receive a properly regulated diet. Today we have a wide choice of first-class 'complete dog meals' all very carefully worked out to give a perfectly balanced diet. I have never found Border Collies to be fussy feeders and have yet to own one that was a bad 'doer'. As most collies will readily polish off any of these complete feeds it is a question of finding out which one suits your dog best. Even when you do find the right one, it is not advisable to keep the dog on it for too long; change his diet now and again. Sometimes these feeds are in the form of a dry meal, in which case it is absolutely imperative to see that the dog has a good supply of fresh water readily available to him; others are in cans or dry packs which need to be moistened. The high cost of these feeds is the one big drawback, but if bought in bulk this can usually be lessened. A word of warning here regarding bulk buying; always be sure it is fresh and in good condition when it arrives and then keep it stored in dry, rat-proof places, preferably in a bin. Meal that has gone mouldy or has weevils in it can make dogs, especially young puppies, very ill. Liver or kidney diseases are carried by rats and are often fatal when contracted by dogs.

A cheaper and more conventional way of feeding dogs is with meat and biscuits or bread, which should always be brown. The meat can be almost any part of any animal, except pork; it is usually offal or tripe depending upon price and supply, but meat in itself is not sufficient as it lacks several essentials; so some additional vitamins and minerals are needed, plus bread or meal for roughage, which is essential for correct bowel action. Many books recommend that bread should always be hard baked for dogs. There is no advantage in this whatever, because as soon as you add milk or gravy, or even a can of meat, you are putting back the moisture you have spent time and fuel on drying out. A hard crust may give the dog pleasure to chew and this is the only advantage as far as I can see, but it is not sufficiently hard to be of any use to help scale the teeth. Some fat is essential in a dog's diet, and the harder a dog works the more he needs, as when it is absorbed into the blood-stream the surplus is stored under the skin around the muscles and helps to act as a kind of lubricant, very necessary for a dog moving as fast as a collie. Fat also helps to lubricate the skin and this in turn nourishes the coat, keeping it glossy and weather-resistant.

Tinned dog meats are a great standby and today's products are of very good quality. Again, they are not cheap, but I prefer to use them rather than cooking and cutting up quantities of paunches (tripes) or struggling with slabs of raw meat. Now that almost every household or kennel has a deep-freeze, kennel blocks of frozen dog meats, minced tripes or even complete frozen feeds are very useful, providing one remembers to take sufficient out to thaw for the next day. Rice and macaroni also make a good nourishing meal but can only be provided if the housewife is willing to cook it. Flaked maize has only limited value for a working dog. Feeding requirements are also governed by climatic and environmental conditions and the correct ration must be in relation to the work load or health of each individual dog. Supplements or any extra vitamins or minerals are usually only necessary on veterinary recommendation in the case of some specific health condition. Note that salt should never be added to a dog's diet, nor should chocolate be given. The salt already in household scraps is permissible, so too is the small amount of chocolate in the covering of those special dog treats, but only if given in strict moderation.

When working, a collie loses a great deal of water from its body through excessive panting; this must be replaced. One often sees collies taking every advantage of a quick drink whenever the opportunity occurs. This is another reason why I am not fully in favour of dry pack types of complete feed, apart from their cost. They cause a dog to drink even more than is normal, and if his stomach is full of water he cannot work properly without pain or stress. Another reason is that it is difficult and expensive to adjust the recommended amounts when, for instance, one is steaming up a bitch prior to whelping or trying to reduce an overindulgent dog without over- or under-feeding the required rations. The sales talk of even the most persuasive representative has not yet fully convinced me to the contrary on this point. All ideas on feeding are really a question of what suits your own particular situation and pocket, and is so often a case of trial and error; but always strive to give the best.

I am often asked if a dog should have one or two meals a day; this very much depends on its work. All my own adult dogs get two meals a day in winter, a light breakfast of bread and milk and their full dinner later. Puppies get three meals a day from approximately four to six months, but if they ever leave anything at any meal then the ration is reduced to two before this age. It never pays to stint on either the quality or quantity of puppy rations.

The question of whether to feed or not to feed dogs before they go out to work can be a problem. I can only answer this in the light of my own experience. In hard weather I think collies should be given a light meal of bread and milk, porridge, or possibly a couple of beaten-up eggs before going out to work; no dog will give of his best if really hungry, and unless his housing conditions are very good he will be hungry by the morning, having used up all the surplus food energy in keeping warm. His main meal can then be given after a brief rest on returning home. This is only my opinion, but any vet will tell you that a dog should never be worked or given strenuous exercise after a big meal; it leads to indigestion at best and bloat at worst. A dog should never be fed when he is really tired; he cannot digest his meal; allow him to have a rest first. The question of feeding before work differs when a dog has to travel or take part in trials or such like, where he works with many more stresses and with much more concentration than on his home ground. In these cases it is wiser to feed him only in the evening.

MATING THE BITCH

The term used for this procedure varies in different parts of the country, and is sometimes referred to as 'lined', 'covered' or 'served', but mating is the most usual term.

While I have found in all other varieties of collies that the dogs and bitches are very co-operative in the 'mating game', the Border Collie dogs are highly selective in the choice of their mates; the bitches, on the other hand, are real little flirts. Men of experience in the sheepdog world are often reluctant to pass on information regarding breeding aspects, not because they wish to keep their knowledge to themselves, but usually because they assume everyone knows all about it, the whole procedure being a matter of routine for them. Descriptions of mating in books most often only mention the bare sequence of events without the details that a novice would wish to know. To be as accurate as possible I made notes for what follows, while each act in the sequence was taking place at my own kennels.

Let us presume you own a Border Collie bitch (registered or unregistered) and you wish to breed with her, but it is your first experience of breeding dogs. To make the experience worthwhile she must have the attributes of the breed, either physical or working, preferably both. If she has not, and is only a beloved family pet, forget the idea as you will be doing no good to yourself or the breed and a replacement when the time comes can be found elsewhere.

As most owners of a bitch know, she comes into season for a period of twenty-one days approximately every six months from about the age of nine months, but the times vary considerably. If she is a family pet and you wish to avoid any temporary inconvenience, then there are alternatives to having her spayed. She can be put on 'the pill' regularly, or given tablets just prior to or at the beginning of a season; a vet will always advise which course of action to take. Should you have the misfortune to have her mated accidentally your vet can give her an injection to avoid conception, but it must be given within forty-eight hours of being mated. This is a little inconvenient sometimes as it prolongs the season for a further three weeks, but even if she is mated again during those three weeks she will not conceive. I myself am not in favour of any

143

of the above methods and prefer to have the bitch spayed if I do not intend to breed; but in all matters concerning the health of your bitch you must be guided by the advice of your own qualified vet.

So now we will assume that your bitch is worthy of being bred from. Your first step should be to study her pedigree or seek the advice of her breeder as to the most suitable stud dog. Most breeders are happy to give this advice and often are even willing to take a puppy or two if they fit in with their own requirements at the time, or they may recommend your litter to prospective customers should they have no pups of their own for sale just then.

Having chosen the stud dog you should then make a tentative booking for his services when you think your bitch is due in season; but it is essential to inform the stud dog owner on the first day the bitch comes on heat, so that he and you can make arrangements for the dog to be available on the day she is due to be mated. This will be on approximately the tenth to thirteenth day of her heat.

Before a bitch is due in season she should be wormed, or at the latest within the first few days of her season. Never worm a bitch during pregnancy, as quite often the worm eggs will find their way through the bloodstream into the pups. All pups have worms even at birth and in my own experience when once or twice I wormed a bitch during pregnancy, as often recommended, the pups were so badly infested with worms that I lost four out of six in one litter when I had to worm them at an early age. After dosing another litter at three weeks on the advice of my vet the effect was devastating; the worms came out from the backs of the eyes, through the nose and up the throat. Luckily I only lost one puppy, but the others were very ill for some time.

Usually the bitch pays great attention to her tail end a day or two before she comes into season (or heat) and on examination you will notice a white discharge from the vulva and after a few days this discharge turns to blood. At approximately the tenth to twelfth day all colour will disappear just for one day, and the vulva will appear very swollen and the surrounding area will be soft and supple. The next day colour will return, but not so strong as before; and this is usually the correct day to mate, when the eggs are shed and ready for fertilization. All this is often very difficult to detect, so 10–13 days are usually considered about the correct time for mating. Every bitch varies considerably in her behaviour at this time. Most bitches continue to show colour for the full three weeks, even after they have been mated, but some clear up within a day or two of being mated. I have not found either way that it affects conception provided she is mated on the right day.

Before the bitch is introduced to the dog give her a run to empty her bladder and bowels, especially if you have come some distance, and see that her tail end is clean. Some dogs will refuse to mate a bitch that is too dirty. This is also unhygienic and can carry some infection either on to the dog or into the bitch. It is a wise precaution to keep the bitch on a lead for the first introduction to watch her reactions. Ideally, if the time is right, she should lift her tail up and to one side while making other flirtatious gestures to the dog, but equally well she can turn on him in no uncertain manner. This may indicate apprehension or that she is not yet ready for mating, or she is playing hard to get. In either case the dog will be able to decide and then he in turn plays the role of hard to get or big bully as he feels the occasion demands.

Next I usually let the bitch off the lead to see which game she is playing. If all is well the dog and bitch have a little preliminary play before he attempts to mount her. After that she should stand and invite him to mount her, but if she still plays hard to get and you know that the dog indicates she is ready, then put her back on the lead and hold her for the dog. Some bitches even need to be muzzled. The owner of the stud dog will know if the dog prefers the bitch held or if he prefers to mate her unattended, so always leave it to the judgement of the stud dog owner to choose if he wants you present at the mating or prefers you to return later for the bitch. Of course you can just let the dog and bitch off their leads in a field and allow natural instincts to take over and all will probably be well; but if you have a long journey to get home and both you and the dog owner have little time to spare, then to have the proceedings under your own control is preferable.

There are many theories on the 'mating game' and each stud dog owner has their own way of coping with this event; but this is my way, as I prefer the whole procedure to be as natural as possible when conditions allow. Once the dog has penetrated, his hind legs will be seen to work up and down very fast while he reaches maximum erection within the bitch. Very occasionally the above procedure (without a tie) will take place outside the bitch due to a last minute manoeuvre by the bitch or by an over-keen or inexperienced dog, and to the casual observer it may appear that the bitch has been covered or mated. This is very frustrating for all concerned and means that several hours may be wasted or possibly that the dog cannot be tried again until the next day. The sperm is then released by a drip feed system. The first few ejaculations before full erection are not usually fertile but the next few are the most important. The bitch and the dog are then fully swollen and what is known as a 'tie' is effected. This may last from five to twenty minutes until the swelling goes down and the bitch then releases the dog. A tie is not necessary for conception provided the dog has stayed inside for sufficient time for those second ejaculations to be effective. I have known dogs to penetrate for only a few moments, yet the bitches had litters; and I have known many dogs who never tie at all. During the tie the dog will turn himself and bring his front legs to one side of the bitch and lift one hind leg over her back in order that he can achieve a more restful position. At this stage it is very important to hold one hand under the bitch in case she should try to sit or lie down. Some bitches are quite silent throughout the proceedings; others make noises from satisfied grunts to positive howling during the whole time. There is no cause for alarm in either case. When dog and bitch eventually part, some bitches will try to turn on the dog while others leap about for joy. Try to restrain both efforts by keeping the bitch on a lead. Give her a drink if she wants one and then put her back in the car to keep quiet. Make sure that no other dog gets to her during the next week or so, as it is perfectly possible for a bitch to conceive to two dogs in one heat. This is one reason why I do not like to have the bitch mated more than once. I once had a bitch mated on the ninth and eleventh days. At the correct time she produced a litter of eight bitch puppies, and two days later she produced a litter of eight dog puppies, all dead. Needless to say, the bitch was very ill, but with the services of my vet she recovered and amazingly never lost her milk and was able to rear the eight bitch pups.

Provided the bitch has been well fed and looked after there is no need to start giving her extra rations or 'steam her up' as they say in farming terms, or to make any alteration to her feeding, exercise or general routine for the first five weeks. Gestation is sixty-three days but can be up to one week earlier and sometimes a few days late. I have always found that at twenty-one to twenty-three days after mating the bitch shows definite signs of pregnancy. Some bitches even suffer from 'morning sickness', others go off their food for several days at intervals during their pregnancy. Her teats will begin to swell, and if she is a maiden they will have a blue ring around them. You can also see and feel that she is swollen just behind the rib cage. After this time, until about two weeks before the litter is due, it is almost impossible to tell if collies are pregnant as they carry the litter so high up in the rib cage.

As collies mature faster than many breeds it is often quite safe to breed from a collie bitch on her first season provided she is over nine months, well developed for her age and in good physical condition. Puppies from young bitches are far healthier and the bitch recovers more quickly. (It must, however, be stressed that she should be well fed, both during the latter part of her pregnancy and during her lactation period.) However, it is sometimes wiser to wait until a bitch and a dog are over two years old before breeding if the question of freedom from P.R.A. is to be taken into account. One could, of course, breed early and not register the pups, selling all as pets. It is up to each owner to decide what course of action to take in this matter.

THE STUD DOG

A golden rule if you want to own a really quick and efficient stud dog is never to chide him, even at an early age, for making any overtures to a bitch. This is as natural to him as it is to a man to 'chat up the girls'. If he is constantly told to 'leave off' he will begin to develop a guilt complex and this is especially true in a Border Collie who responds so quickly to any form of discipline. So it is very important to give a young dog encouragement to establish his confidence as the bitch is usually quite capable of putting him in his place should he overstep the mark. Correct feeding and exercise also play an important part, as an under-nourished (this does not necessarily mean underfed) and over- or under-exercised dog cannot make a satisfactory stud dog. Inci-dentally, some prefer to call them stallion dogs, but this term as a rule only applies to hounds.

It is usually more convenient for matings to take place in the evenings, so it is advisable merely to give the dog a light breakfast and withhold his evening meal until he has performed. I make this point because some dogs, unless extremely keen, will not give full attention to the job if they are hungry, and this is where the earlier breakfast can have helped. I once had a really keen stud dog who would refuse to serve a bitch if she came at his usual dinner time. He demanded his dinner, got it, and then carried on with the job—but I have always found it an advantage not to keep them too hungry. With regard to exercise, if a dog has to do a full day's work he should be given a good rest before being asked to perform, because if the bitch proves difficult he may have to con-tinue his pursuit for a couple of hours before he wins her over. On the other hand if it is a slack period and the dog has not been out much it is advisable to give him a good run to help him empty himself and generally tone him up.

Most Border Collie dogs will be in demand for their potential as sires of good working stock, so the colour or texture of their coat will be of no consequence to the bitch owners, but pet owners are usually more concerned with the good looks of the dog. Regarding the texture of the coat, this can be either rough or smooth and either variety can appear in the same litter, but the smooth dog is not so popular as a sire where the pet owner is concerned. I know this from experience having owned stud dogs of both coats.

Here is some information regarding colour inheritance, without going into the details of chromosomes, etc. Two black-and-whites will produce black-and-white or tricolours, depending on the colours of their ancestors. Two tricolours will only produce tricolours. These are mainly black with the usual white markings plus tan eyebrows and cheek markings and also tan inside the hind legs. Tricolour mated to a black-and-white can produce both colours and also black-and-tan and sometimes a sable or brown-and-white. Tricolour mated with a blue merle will produce both tricolour and blue merle. This information is derived from standard literature on colour inheritance, but all rules have their exceptions and I have known Border Collies that have disproved some of these theories.

It will be appreciated that in the following paragraphs I am writing in the main about any stud dog. In the sheepdog world it is probably wiser to wait until a dog has had some training for his farm work before using him at stud. This is a matter upon which each sheepdog owner will have his own views. If a dog proves useless for work, then there is little point in breeding with him, while on the other hand sometimes a dog tried at stud later in life is either unable or unwilling to perform his task.

A dog may be tried for stud work after the age of ten months and if he is ready and can effect a mating you can assume you have an efficient stud. The young dog should not be used again for at least three months. If he is not ready, the experience of having played and courted a bitch, provided she is a willing partner, will have been all to the good. The number of times or frequency that a dog can be used at stud varies with the demands for his stock. A very popular dog is often used once a week; I feel this is more than sufficient but may be unavoidable at certain times of the year. A dog really well fed and cared for is capable of siring a litter until he is ten or twelve years old, but his stock will not be so good or healthy after about eight years old. My wonderful Highland collie sired his last litter when he was sixteen years old; the bitch was young and it was a very good litter, but this was an exceptional case. Should a dog have been a successful sire at the tender age of ten months or so and there is a resulting litter, then the dog can be said to be a proved sire and a stud fee fixed according to his merits. It is unusual to charge a stud fee for a dog's first service, but the owner can request a puppy in return if he so desires. This is an optional matter which differs with each owner. With a proved stud dog his fee should be requested at the time of service. I do not give a Kennel Club registered dog's pedigree until the owner of the bitch informs me of details regarding any resulting litter, but I do give a receipt for the service with all relevant details and whelping date. For a dog registered with the International Sheep Dog Society a mating card must be filled in and one part returned to the Society within fourteen days, and the other part of the card is given to the bitch owner.

The actual mating procedure has already been described, but I should mention here a very new form of service which is now proving very successful—this is artificial insemination. Farmers have been familiar for years with the benefits of A.I. in other live-stock, but with dogs it has only just started, and so far only a few litters have been born as a result of these tests. We are fortunate in this country that we have some of the best sheepdogs in the world with which to mate our bitches, and all within a day's travelling distance. Flockmasters in other parts of the world could benefit greatly from this new technique as they could have the services of an outstanding dog without the expense of importa-tion, quarantine, etc., to say nothing of the cost of the dog—always providing the owner was even willing to sell.

Very briefly, the procedure is as follows. The dog is taken to an approved centre for blood and other tests, then a sperm specimen is taken. It is then transferred to a suitable medium and container for freezing to keep it at the right condition for a given length of time. It is then sent, usually by air, to the veterinary practitioner who is to perform the implant. At present the use of this technique is very limited, and the person wishing to import the semen must make application to the correct government department in his own country (in some cases this may never be granted); they must then find a private or departmental vet willing or approved to carry out the implant. Next an export and health certificate must be obtained from the correct department in this country. So almost a year can pass before all the documents and so on are ready; then the importer must wait for the bitch to come into season and hope he can get her to the right place at the right time. At first the Kennel Club refused registration of litters born as a result of A.I. as they wished to protect owners of registered dogs from any possible malpractices. However, with their new registration system, which is more in line with that of the International Sheep Dog Society, the Kennel Club now accept these litters for full registration, under certain circumstances where such a decision is absolutely vital. For any further information on this matter it would be advisable to contact the International Sheep Dog Society as matters such as these are constantly altering due to some new regulation or experiment.

It is always a debatable point whether a dog or a bitch has the most influence on a breed, but because of the number of his services I feel the dog has the advantage here, so it is vital that he is not used at stud if he is known to have any hereditary faults. A bitch may have only one litter and with luck all the progeny may take after her if she is free from hereditary defects; if you have not been lucky she need not be bred from again. However, the dog may sire many litters before anything is discovered, so the testing of a stud dog for P.R.A. is of the utmost importance here.

CARE OF THE PREGNANT BITCH

The care of a pregnant or lactating working collie bitch is an area where much abuse of this breed occurs. Perhaps the new Dog

Breeders Act (requirements of the Act are quoted elsewhere), if it can be properly implemented, will help to stamp out the unnecessary suffering this causes.

True shepherds know the value of their stock and their dogs are very rarely ill-treated, but some are not so considerate, regarding all forms of livestock as disposable material to be kept for work and financial gain only. I know of several cases where a farmer has worked his bitch up to the day she whelped without giving her any extra rations. Such a bitch, by virtue of her survival at all under the conditions in which she is kept, is a very healthy one, and usually whelps her litter safely, but she has to feed them off her own back, which results in an almost emaciated bitch at the time of weaning and puppies that have a poor start in life. I have bought puppies at the age of four weeks from these sources in order to relieve the bitch and give the litter a better start. Needless to say the transaction subsequently proved very costly. When I tried to point out this lack of consideration to the farmer I was rudely told to mind my own business and I had no idea what I was talking about! Another case of sheer thoughtlessness—to put it politely—which I encountered was that of a bitch who had to whelp while still chained up. She was a wonderful worker with the most delightful nature in spite of the treatment she had received on the farm, and for this reason I had booked a puppy from her. When I went to the farm a few days after the puppies were due I found her still on a chain nursing four puppies in a filthy wet kennel in a muddy yard. She came out to greet me in her usual way, her whole body wriggling along the ground with pleasure. It was pouring with rain and she had to return into the kennel to nurse her litter, covered with mud. The farmer told me she had eight pups one night and the next morning he put all of them outside the kennel and waited to see which four she brought back first as he only wanted this number. Here was a classic case of the survival of the fittest. I felt very upset and depressed about the state of the bitch and her litter but decided this time to mind my own business until I could think of a remedy. When I went to collect my pup I persuaded the farmer to sell me the bitch as well, and he agreed because he said she was in too poor a condition to work! I still have the pup, and her picture as an adult (Plate 14a) appears in this book with her own litter born and reared under very different circumstances. I kept the dam for a time to build her up properly and then gave her to an old age pensioner where she lives in the lap of luxury as she rightly deserves.

It may seem unnecessary to keep referring to the unkind, almost cruel treatment meted out to these collies in the past and even still on some farms today, but this is part of the history of the breed, without which the story would be incomplete. The above episodes serve as examples of the lack of care which in turn is a reason for so many poor specimens of Border Collie one encounters. Consequently I am always very suspicious when I read 'farm bred or reared' in advertisements.

Let us now consider the happier side of things and the proper care the bitch should be given during this period. A pregnant bitch can be used for work until about her last two weeks as by this time she will be getting heavy, probably carrying an extra 10 lbs. for an average litter of six. The extra bulk will cause a strain on her heart, stomach and kidneys which she is well adapted to cope with under normal conditions. She should be given reasonable exercise at this stage and the food can be reduced in quantity but not in quality.

WHELPING QUARTERS

If these quarters are to be somewhere outside, then the place should be draughtproof, dry and as quiet as possible. A large tea chest is an ideal bed or nest, but it should have an extra floor inside; chipboard well sealed is ideal. If making a new box for the purpose this type is as good as any; the size should be approximately 18 in. longer and wider than the bitch when she is stretched out asleep. If the bed is too big a newborn puppy can be pushed too far away from the bitch while she is asleep or attending to the others, and it may get cold and die; but if the bed is too small the puppies can get crushed when the mother is turning round or,

153

when they are a little older, they can get pushed out of the nest in the scramble for the milk bar. A hinged flap, also of chipboard, approximately 6 in. high, across the base of the front of the open side of the box is useful for keeping draughts out and puppies in, and can be let down to provide a ramp when they get to the crawling about stage; if the flap is kept up when they reach this stage they often fall out and are unable to get back.

A guard rail around the inside of the box is often suggested in order to eliminate the possibility of puppies getting crushed. I am not in favour of this as it is uncomfortable for the bitch and, in fact, as far as I can see, has no advantages at all. At the time when the pups are most likely to get crushed they would not be capable of moving out into this area; at a later date, when they are stronger, they will be capable of getting out from under the bitch should she lie on one. I find it better to keep a watch on the nest now and then for the first few days—if the nest is within earshot it is only too easy to hear if anything is amiss.

Tack a piece of blanket or sacking firmly across the top of the open side of the box so that it can be turned back to lie on the top; this facilitates inspection of the litter after it is born. Put several layers of newspaper into the box and leave the bitch to have fun making a nest in it. Always make sure that a bowl of fresh water is near the bed—I really do mean fresh, as bitches get very thirsty during pregnancy and lactation and dislike drinking stale or dusty water at this time.

A good light is essential and some form of safe heating in the shed or kennel is a great advantage. Leaving a light on at night for the first few nights after the litter is born helps the bitch to see what she is doing. Dogs may have a wonderful sense of smell and a great deal of instinct, but they can't see in the dark. The question of heating is one that always sparks off a lot of controversy. Personally I do not think it is always necessary to have heat in the shed or kennel providing the nest is really warm and comfortable. There is no doubt that the warmer one can keep the bitch the better central heating she can provide in the nest; much depends upon the time of year, but it is far more important to keep the place dry. I have never used infra-red lamps as I have a theory that they do more harm than good. If you were to take the temperature of the nest box at the level of the floor of the box and again at about the height of the head of the bitch when she is sitting up, you would find that at floor level it is considerably cooler if a lamp is used. These lamps tend to draw up the cold air at the floor level and keep the nest constantly cooler just where heat is needed most. It is more likely that the lamps will provide the heat to the bitch only, who in all probability will find this too exhausting. Most bitches also prefer the nest box to be dark and find the constant light an irritation. So I prefer to keep the whole nest box warm and let the bitch provide the extra heat for the pups. Even the dull emitter types of lamp have the same cooling effects on the floor area.

If the bitch is to whelp indoors then a quiet spot must be selected away from the usual household disturbances. All mine are whelped indoors mainly for my own convenience as I have heat and light all ready to hand. I have been breeding collies of all varieties for over thirty years and I am still using the same whelping bed or nest box. The number of puppies born in this bed now runs into three figures. It has a removable floor which has been replaced several times. I consider a really good bed either for sleeping or whelping as a wise investment, if you intend to breed dogs. It must be thoroughly scrubbed and disinfected before and after each litter. If whelping outdoors then a bed made from straw bales is excellent, but is only economical if you have a farm. If you do settle for this type of bed, it needs a wooden floor, because a flooring of straw can force the bitch to eat some of it while she is performing any cleaning up operations either during whelping or when the puppies get older. Breeders' theories on this subject are endless and there is no doubt that one must be guided by the facilities that are available in one's own particular home; but my own requirements may be of some help to a complete novice.

WHELPING

Whelping is the correct term for a bitch giving birth and the puppies are referred to as whelps. They cease to be whelps and become known as pups when they are weaned. Collies, even the show variety, are more disposed to natural whelping than a number of other breeds, as man has interfered relatively little with their body structure from behind the head. I propose to give details of a normal whelping as I feel strongly that should there be any doubts or complications the vet is the right person to deal with them. Many breeders with experience in dealing with livestock will be able to cope adequately in these situations and will have no need of advice from me, but these chapters are intended for novice breeders, and even a normal whelping may be a frightening experience when encountered for the first time.

There are several schools of thought on the subject of whelping. There are those who shut the pregnant bitch up each night and hope to find her happy and contented with a litter of pups next morning, as indeed is very often the case; but you must be a fairly relaxed sort of person to subscribe to this procedure. There are several other types of owner, down to the one who fusses and gets in a flap, sending for a vet before labour pains have even begun and generally upsetting themselves, the bitch and the vet.

Let us presume that you are one of those owners who feel the bitch knows best (and she usually does). You know that she likes you to be on hand to give praise and comfort for going through a process which was your wish, not hers, in most cases. I am not the flappable type but I like to be present when my bitches are whelping just in case of necessity.

During the latter part of the bitch's pregnancy you may notice a colourless discharge from the vulva which is quite normal and usually indicates that all is well for an easy whelping. If it has a reddish tinge, keep a watch on her, and if it is dark green or black take her along to the vet. You will also note that she will lose most of the hair on the underside of her body so that the teats are quite free. Always give her a good grooming to remove all dead coat and have her really clean, especially at the tail end. A few days before the litter is due I always wipe the teats with an oil-soaked cloth to get them clean and supple so that the pups have the best start possible.

Sometimes about a week before the whelping date the bitch will go off her food and seem restless. If she is given the opportunity she will roll about a lot on the grass and have a grand time making a nest by tearing up the paper in her bed. All this display is quite usual, but often alerts one into thinking she is about to start labour. This is when I rush for the thermometer. If her temperature is normal and all is well then I know that I can have another night's sleep, as bitches usually decide to whelp at night when all is quiet. However, if her temperature has gone below normal I keep watch and take it again in a few hours' time. When she is due to whelp the temperature usually goes down to between 90°–100°. In the meanwhile I put down her dinner which she usually eats; if she does, I assume that the display was a false alarm, and that she was just having a rehearsal. If this is the case, then the litter will usually arrive on the sixty-third day. Border Collies can be as unpredictable in this matter as the sheep they tend, and I have been taken in on several occasions; the bitch, having shown no sign of any temperature alteration, has eaten a meal, then retired to bed and within a short time I have been greeted by faint cries and have found her with one or more live squirming little wet black slugs in the nest.

When the female of the species starts in labour there are three definite stages:

1. Bed-making and first strains or contractions.
2. The production of the young.
3. The production of the afterbirth, but with multiviparious animals such as bitches, stages 2 and 3 are combined or sometimes alternate.

At the first onset of labour the bitch will be very restless, panting, wanting to go out and then coming indoors again quickly, or she will have a fine time tearing up the bedding. At this stage take little notice of her except to give her every opportunity to relieve herself outside, as you may not be able to persuade her to leave her puppies for anything up to twenty-four hours once they are born.

In the final stages of labour the water bag will appear; sometimes this is broken before it appears, very little pushing or straining being noticeable at this stage, but as contractions increase the bitch will then either lie down to strain or stand up, and sometimes even walk about. If no puppy appears within two hours and the bitch is still straining, or a puppy has appeared but she cannot deliver it, then send for a vet. Usually a puppy will appear within twenty minutes of contractions or quite soon after they start. Each puppy arrives encased in a sac of liquid with the afterbirth attached by the umbilical cord.

As soon as the pup is dropped (most collies produce their puppies from a standing position) the bitch will bite open the bag and proceed to eat the afterbirth while cutting the cord, all apparently at the same time. Sometimes a bitch is not quite sure what to do with her first puppy; if you break the bag for her and then rub the puppy briskly with a towel and make it squeal, this will bring her maternal instincts into play. It is remarkable how from then onwards the bitch seems to go into what one can only describe as a complete whelping routine with each arrival. This whole process can take all night or it can be over in a matter of a couple of hours, depending upon the length of time between each arrival, and the number of them. The vigorous licking given to each pup by the bitch stimulates it to enable it to pass water or a motion, which it cannot do otherwise. Do not be upset at the apparently rough treatment she will give her puppies; this is stimulating procedure and a part of the routine. I like to remove each pup as soon as the next one is being born and put it in a small box with a piece of blanket wrapped around a hot water bottle, as often a pup can get trodden or laid on when the bitch is attending to the next arrival. Some bitches will not allow you to do this or even put your hand near the pups, but most like to be relieved of the responsibility for a while. When I think all the litter have arrived and the mother has settled down to a good sleep with the last one or two sucking away happily, then I give her back the rest, putting them on the teats if possible. It is amazing how each pup seems to claim one particular teat, and you will find it very difficult to persuade it to start off at any other one. When each has had its fill from its own teat then there is a general post. When the bitch is satisfied that the pups are clean and dry she will try to get a good rest.

Some breeders offer the bitch a warm milk drink after whelping, but I prefer to give her glucose and water. She will still be in a shocked state and if she has eaten all the afterbirths her digestive juices will have enough to cope with, but the glucose will help her recovery. While she is resting, try very carefully to remove as much soiled newspaper as possible and replace it if you can. Be sure to take it away and burn it as soon as possible. If it is left around you may find her out of bed later on searching through it for a pup she thinks may be there. Then pull the blanket down over the opening and if the whelping quarters are outside and the conditions very cold put another blanket over the whole bed, making sure you have left some space for ventilation, preferably down the side of the bed; leave the bitch in peace, preferably with a light on, to look after her new family.

You should inspect the milk bar after a few days, and if the area around any of the teats seems hard and swollen, give a gentle massage and try to put the strongest pups on to it to reduce the build-up of milk; as the strongest pups are usually the greediest they will not be too fussy where their extra rations come from, and this will give the bitch great relief. If the hardening is ignored it may even turn to mastitis, and in any case as it causes the bitch pain she may sometimes turn on the pups with fatal consequences.

This should be sufficient to help a novice breeder without going into details about complications that may never occur. My experience with whelping Border Collies has been that they are quite capable of conducting their own confinements. There is, however, one condition which may occur in the bitch at any time from twenty-four hours to three days after whelping; it is happily very rare, but if it is not spotted at once the bitch will die. This is called eclampsia, or milk fever. It is caused by most of the calcium in the bitch's body having been drained away by the litter. No amount of calcium given to the bitch during pregnancy will prevent it, although this may be beneficial in other ways. It can be overcome by a massive dose of calcium given by a vet direct into the bloodstream. The recovery after this injection is miraculous; an almost dead bitch can appear to be quite normal again within half-an-hour in some cases. As I have said, eclampsia is a rare occurrence, but it is well to be able to recognize the symptoms. The bitch will appear extremely upset, not knowing where to put herself. She will pant abnormally and in the latter stages will lie out quite stiff. The vet must be sent for at once, and told that you suspect this condition so that he can bring the necessary dose. Take the pups away and put them in a box with either a blanket or plenty of newspaper and keep them warm, as the mother may crush them when in this distressed condition.

Warmth, especially that derived from close contact with the bitch, is of paramount importance to the new-born pup. The drying-out process reduces the body temperature which can be compensated by the bitch's licking, but she cannot attend to all the new arrivals at once. Often a really good mother will tuck one or two up under her tail until she has time to deal with them later. Keep the bitch on a light diet for the first two days after whelping, as her stomach will still be full. You may find that when the after-births have been digested the bitch is inclined to have diarrhoea for a day or two. Some breeders like to stop the bitch from eating the afterbirth on the grounds that it may cause vomiting or choking.

The next day you should try to clean the bitch up if her coat is soiled, as this can bring back infection to the litter. At the same time—in fact in any case—you should examine the bitch to make sure all is well and note if she has a slight discharge. This is normal and may last from one to six weeks. If it is not present, it may mean a dead puppy or an afterbirth has been retained or that she has some infection in the womb. Take her temperature and if it is not normal send for the vet. If it is normal and the bitch is taking some food there is no need to worry as it may come right next day.

Many breeders automatically have a post-whelping check by a vet, to make sure the whelping is really over; as part of his check he will give the bitch an injection of antibiotic and pituitary extract as a prevention against any post-parturient metritis. It is sometimes difficult to keep a note of whether all the afterbirths have come away, and this will make sure.

There may not appear to be much milk at first, just the thick sticky colostrum which is essential, but the milk supply will increase as the strength of the pups increases, and so too will the bitch's appetite. She should be having three full meals a day at the end of the first week. I like to start weaning the puppies at about four weeks to lessen the drain on the bitch, and when the pups begin on solid food I reduce her rations. I have always found that when she sees me feeding them she reduces her milk supply or sometimes refuses to feed them, while giving you a look as much as to say 'you can take over now'! As the pups begin to move about you will notice that she feeds them standing up. This is to get them up on their legs and make them strong, but you need to watch that if there is a little one amongst them he can reach up to get his share. It may be necessary to hold him up until he gets a good grip on his own particular teat.

Border Collies are also wonderful foster-mothers and used to be in great demand by the big breeding kennels for fostering orphaned litters or in cases where a bitch had more puppies than she could feed. At one time it was quite usual to see advertisements in farming and country journals offering collie foster-mothers. Today many pet-food manufacturers produce various aids and foods for hand-rearing orphaned puppies, but however sophisticated these may be it still means three- to four- hourly administrations by the breeders, to say nothing of the topping and tailing or bed cleaning.

REARING THE PUPPIES

Puppies are born deaf and blind and remain so until they are
about ten days old, when the most forward ones will open their
eyes; all in the litter will be open by two weeks. Hearing is gained
a little later and as I explained in the chapter on training, the
first sounds registering in the puppies' brains are their first contact with human beings and the new world. Although their eyes
are open they cannot focus or see properly for another week or so.

Personally I do not have the dew claws removed from collies
unless they appear on the hind legs, but I do for the smooth show
collies, as it improves the clean appearance of the legs for the
show ring but if you wish to have them removed this should be
done by a vet at three to five days old. The puppies should have
their nails cut when approximately three weeks old, as these can
tear the dam and cause her great pain, especially when she feeds
them in the standing-up position. Fig. 4 shows the correct way
to cut nails, and any ordinary sharp scissors or nail clippers is all
that is needed for this job.

If a bitch refuses to feed the pups when they are about two
weeks old or starts to feed them and then gets up, it often means
that they are hurting her with their needle-sharp teeth. In this case
it is wise just to nip off the tips of the milk teeth, thus blunting
them a little—it does not affect the teeth in any way. Any operation
of this nature must be performed when the dam is well out of earshot, as any unnatural squeals will upset her. In any case, even if
you have only used her absence to clean out the bedding, the litter
will be subjected to a mammoth inspection and clean-up on her
return.

I worm the pups at approximately four weeks or when I think
they have built up a lining to their intestines and can digest some
solid food. Each puppy is weighed on old kitchen scales and dosed
according to the instructions on whatever vermicide is given, with
a further dose ten to fourteen days later.

Up to this stage the bitch has had the responsibility of rearing

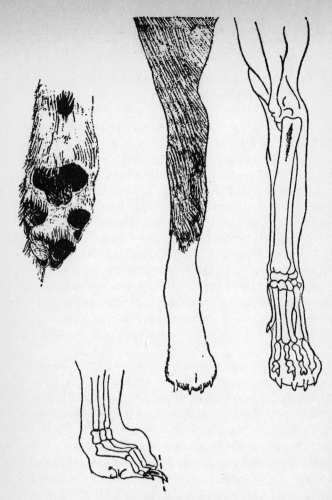

Fig. 4 Feet

These should be oval in shape with soles well padded, toes arched and close together. The hind feet are slightly less arched. Good feet and legs are essential to all dogs; strength and shape are determined by the work for which they are bred.

The left half of the foot untrimmed. The right half of the foot correctly trimmed.

Nails should be kept short. The dotted line indicates the angle to cut, taking care to avoid nipping the quick. Finally, gently use a nail file to give a smooth finish.

the puppies, with supervision from the breeder, but now it is your turn to take over. There may be some circumstances such as illness, or accident, or the bitch simply refusing to feed them any longer, when the breeder will have to take over completely right from the start. If a foster mother cannot be found, a word of warning here regarding feeding. In these cases baby foods or milks are not sufficient to replace the bitch's milk, as they are made up of ingredients intended for a different digestive system, and a much slower growth rate. To maintain steady growth in the puppies and to supply all the nourishment needed, it is essential that the breeder feeds properly prepared food intended for puppy rearing. Litters that have lacked the bitch's milk at an early stage and have been reared by the breeders on baby foods or cow's milk never catch up with litters that have been reared by the bitch until at least four weeks, and then weaned on meat plus baby foods. This is not an advertisement for puppy-rearing foods, but knowledge I have gained from my own experience with many litters.

If hand-rearing becomes necessary, then provided the puppies can obtain the colostrum found in the bitch's milk during the first few days and are later put on to puppy-rearing milk food, the litter does not suffer quite such a setback. For this operation a premature baby bottle teat is advisable, depending on age of course. The ordinary baby bottle teat might be too big for very young Border Collie puppies. It is important to remember that hand-reared puppies must have their tummies and rectum gently massaged with a soft damp cloth after each feed to stimulate action of the kidneys and bowels. Sometimes an obliging older dog or bitch will help out with this topping and tailing job. Very young puppies are unable to perform this operation for themselves without this stimulation.

At approximately four weeks, earlier if the pups are very forward or becoming a drain on the dam, I try each one with a little raw minced meat in the folded palm of my hand. They like to get their noses up against your flesh and push the meat into their own mouths rather than you having to put it in, but sometimes you can help by edging a little of the meat into the side of the mouth. Again this first contact with something new and pleasant, an association with your hand, is another area where confidence in human relationship is being established. No puppy really likes to have its nose rammed into a bowl of milk or baby food. It usually backs away at once, choking and sneezing, even if the experience proves pleasant later. The mince is given once the first day, twice the next day, then three times a day for the first week of weaning—approximately one teaspoonful per pup at each feed, gradually increasing the amount.

The best time to feed the litter is when the dam is out at exercise, so that she cannot see you doing it. The puppies are, of course, still having the full ration of milk from her. The following week I add baby food or special puppy meal morning and evening, mixed with milk, or according to the maker's instruction, plus raw or cooked meat at midday. By this time you will notice that the dam wants to feed them less and to be with them less often.

Many breeders like to start off weaning their pups by giving them milk and baby foods first, teaching them to lap. My theory is that they are already getting sufficient of the nourishment that the dam's milk supplies and need something more substantial by this time. Also, by introducing these extras you are getting the pups' digestive systems slowly used to them. Either method can be followed or you can use one of those ready-prepared complete puppy diets that are on the market. These are excellent, if a little costly, and certainly take a lot of guessing out of feeding a litter.

About the fifth week I keep the dam away from the litter for most of the day, except for a brief visit morning and evening if she wishes to feed them, and then I only allow her a few minutes with them. This helps her to dry off without any uncomfortable build-up of milk, as the less that is drawn off the less she will make.

By this time the litter should be on four meals a day. Increase the size of the meals gradually by approximately a tablespoonful per pup each week. Overfeeding will cause sickness and diarrhoea. Watch the litter feeding, as sometimes one little chap gets pushed out or keeps running from place to place, and in this way he usually misses out while his brothers and sisters are getting their heads down until they are full. For this reason I like to feed a litter in the type of round dish illustrated (Plate 1a). However hard they push each other they are forced to keep going round, and this way all get a fair share. If there is one small pup then I give him an extra saucer of food somewhere else when the others have finished. It is surprising how quickly they come to know this and expect it, rushing off to that special place as soon as the trough is empty.

If you do not already have bookings for the puppies it is advisable to advertise them at about five weeks old, giving full details. Should a customer definitely book one which is not ready to go yet, then take a deposit on it, and make sure to take the name and address; the safest place is on the stub of the receipt. If the customer cancels the puppy later, giving you a really satisfactory explanation, then you should return the deposit, but if they have caused you inconvenience by not coming for the pup at the arranged date and you have missed another sale for it in the meantime I think it is only fair that you should keep at least some of the deposit, depending on the amount and the extra length of time you have had to keep the pup. Always be able to supply full details regarding the date of birth, pedigree and transfer form if the puppy is registered with the International Sheep Dog Society, diet sheet plus sufficient food for at least two meals, so that the diet is not changed too quickly.

Mainly for the Pet Owner

There are many excellent books or leaflets giving advice on how to look after your new puppy, and the pet owner can gain much information by reading the whole of this chapter, but always make sure that your dog, especially if a young puppy, has a supply of fresh water available at all times. Like all young things, puppies are very thirsty creatures. Dogs will quite happily drink what appears to us to be dirty muddy water from a pool or pond, but will not drink stale or dust-contaminated tap water that has been chlorinated. It is a wise precaution to bring a bottle of water from home for a young puppy if you plan to take him out with you for a day. Water (except rain water) from another district can sometimes upset puppies in the same way as it can babies. Personally I always have a plastic bottle of water and an old plastic dish in the car whenever I take the dogs out, also a damp cloth in a plastic bag, and some newspapers for any emergencies in mopping-up operations.

In the wild state a bitch would begin to wean her pups by regurgitating a meal for them so that the food would be already partly digested, and this process would continue until the pups were old enough to go out and hunt for their own food. I have had two bitches who would always do this for the pups; one would regurgitate the food I had given her and the other would go out hunting and catch game, rabbits or field mice. She once killed a whole nest of young pheasants and brought one a day back for her pups until the nest was empty.

The next step in the growing partnership between you and your collie is his training, and I should like to make an observation here. Your puppy was born with a certain personality which he will possess all his life, but the formation of his general character will, through training and association with you, reflect some of your personality as well. It is very true to say that some dogs are like their owners; see to it that this is a compliment in your own case. The choice and opportunity lie with you.

Chapter 5

THE WORLD OF DOG SHOWS

In the bizarre world of dog shows, the three Rs mean Registrations, Rules and Regulations and success should never be measured by the awards gained but by the satisfaction and enjoyment given and received with involvement in this sport or hobby. I frankly admit that up to a few years ago I was convinced that working collies had no place in the show ring and I am still of that opinion when one is considering just the working dog. However, we are now considering a pure-bred pedigree dog fully recognized as a Border Collie and used for many other purposes, and I now entirely agree with this new freedom of choice which means that we can do what we wish, within the law, with the breed we have chosen, a privilege hitherto denied to owners of Border Collies outside the world of shepherding and obedience. This chapter is written for all those who wish to show their Border Collie, but who have no previous experience of the show world.

REGISTRATIONS

When a breed becomes eligible for the show ring, it is necessary that the intended exhibit is registered at the Kennel Club, either by the breeder or the owner, before it can be shown or exhibited at shows where Kennel Club rules apply. However, in the case of the Border Collie we are once more faced with an odd situation. As the Kennel Club regulations stand at present, these dogs can

The World of Dog Shows

only be accepted for registration if they are already registered with the International Sheep Dog Society, but this Society only recognizes the Border Collie in its capacity as a sheepdog; one is left wondering how long this situation can continue. Further, to register a litter or a dog one must first become a member of the Society and only dogs of already registered parents can be accepted, except under certain conditions. Finally, only litters from parents who have passed the P.R.A. tests are now eligible for registration except at double fees. This to me seems a very wise condition, if a little frustrating and costly to the owners. One can only admire the Society for sticking to its principles and their right to do so must be accepted.

If you want to purchase a Border Collie, or already own one that you wish to show, make sure that you have its International Sheep Dog Society official registration number certificate, which must be applied for by the breeder, but can bear your name as the owner, thus saving a transfer fee. Fill these particulars in on the Kennel Club application form for registration, which can be obtained from 1 Clarges Street, London W1Y 8AB, and send it together with the fee quoted. It will be entered on the Basic Register, and it is then necessary to apply to have it transferred to the Active Register if you wish to show the dog within six months. In due course you will receive back your registration card, and it is the particulars on this card only which you quote when filling in your entry forms for shows. The same procedure applies if you wish to enter a Border Collie in the Obedience Register of the Kennel Club. The Kennel Club, founded in 1873 by Mr Shirley from Gloucestershire, a well-known collie and gundog breeder, is the governing body of all registered pedigree dogs in the United Kingdom and all shows are held under their rules and regulations, with the exception of Exemption Shows; although these are licensed by the Kennel Club, its rules and regulations do not apply to them. You do not need to be a member in order to register a dog. Once you have fulfilled these requirements, your Border Collie is eligible for the show ring and it only remains for you to produce him in the best possible physical condition, and well-groomed. It is hoped that the complete novice will find my hints on showing and preparation useful, but no amount of reading will compensate for practical experience.

Dog shows as we know them today first started in Newcastle in June of 1859 with pointers and setters only scheduled. Previously these were in the form of open days and trials held for gundogs and terriers. The first dog show to schedule sheepdogs was held in Birmingham in December 1860. Of course these sheepdogs were a very mixed bag and included any type of farming or herding dog. In classes for these dogs at Darlington Show in 1868 the schedule advertised classes for 'shepherd's dogs' for male, and 'cur bitches' for female classes.

TYPES OF SHOWS

Here below is a list of the various types of shows held under Kennel Club rules, but I will first explain a little more about Exemption Shows. These are small local affairs usually run in conjunction with fêtes or gymkhanas. The first four classes are devoted to pedigree dogs and are judged according to Kennel Club rules. Other classes are for fun only, in which both pedigree and mongrel dogs can be entered. These provide an excellent opportunity for a 'first-timer', but take great care of your dog as some of the non-pedigree dogs are not as well-behaved or disciplined as those one meets in the official show ring. I have judged as many as twenty so-called Border Collies entered in the various non-pedigree classes at these shows and there have often been the same number entered in the obedience section, but with no standard to guide me I awarded the prizes to those I considered most typical, including their general behaviour.

Sanction Shows

All exhibitors must be *bona fide* members of the association, club or society holding the show. The number of scheduled classes is restricted, and dogs which have won Challenge Certificates may not compete or if they have won over a certain number of awards, thus giving better advantage to new members and new dogs.

Limited Shows

No dog which has won a Challenge Certificate can be entered at this class of show either. Limited shows are restricted to members of clubs or societies, or to exhibitors within specified areas.

Open Shows

As the word implies, the classes are open to dogs of members, or non-members, members usually paying entry fees at a reduced rate. Challenge Certificate winners and champions can also enter, as there is no restriction on the number of awards won.

Championship Shows

These are a combination of classes scheduled at all the above, plus the award of Challenge Certificates to the best dog and best bitch (see *The Challenge Certificate* overleaf).

A Benched Show

This is one where niches raised off the ground provide accommodation for your dog while at the show; small rings are provided to which the dog can be secured, and a wire mesh above to hold the ring number, prize cards, and if you wish, your kennel name. Dogs must not be away from their benches for more than fifteen minutes at any one time during a show except when in the ring or being exercised.

Unbenched Shows

Exhibitors must find what accommodation they can around the hall for themselves and the dogs.

The Challenge Certificate

This is the highest award at a championship show. The dog or bitch must have taken first place in all the classes for which it has been entered. It then challenges all the other unbeaten dogs or bitches in the breed that day. The overall winner in each sex is awarded the Challenge Certificate and then goes on to challenge for Best of Breed on the day. The eventual winner goes on to represent the breed in the grand ring. Three Challenge Certificates won under three different judges, providing the dog is over one year old, give it the title of 'Champion'. The number of sets of certificates are all allocated by the Kennel Club to canine societies according to the number of entries in the breed at the various championship shows. This is just a brief summary but will be sufficient here. I hope the first Border Collie to be made champion in the show ring comes from good working stock. It is my dearest wish that this dog or bitch may have had the magic words 'I.S.D.S. International' or even 'National Champion' in front of its name.

JUDGES AND EXHIBITORS

To exhibit, all one needs is a dog, the initial courage and duly completed entry form, but to judge one needs not only a mental picture of the correct type according to the Breed Standard but also a full knowledge of how that particular breed is constructed beneath the skin and how each part functions in connection with the type of work it has to perform. Since the information given here is purely for the novice, I did not feel it necessary to include separate illustrations of the bone and muscle structure of the breed but the illustration (see Fig. 5) may be helpful. The mental picture built up by each judge from the Kennel Club Interim Breed Standard will vary; so too will each judge place greater emphasis on certain aspects of the breed. A specialist judge tends to regard the head as of supreme importance, while an all-rounder (someone who judges a number of breeds) may consider that the general all-round balance and appearance is more important. That

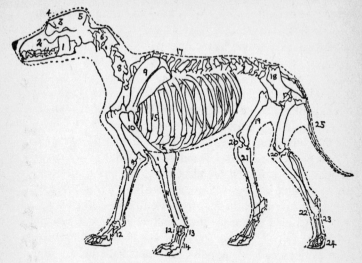

Fig. 5 Skeleton of a Border Collie

1. Lower jaw (mandible); 2. Upper jaw (maxilla); 3. Cranium;
4. Stop; 5. Occiput; 6,7,8. Cervical vertebrae; 9. Shoulder blade
(scapula); 10. Humerus and elbow joint; 11. Forearm (radious);
12. Carpal bones; 13. Position of stopper pad; 14. Pasterns (meta-
carpels); 15. Ribs; 16. Sternum; 17. Thoracic and lumbar vertebrae;
18. Pelvis and hip joint; 19. Femur; 20. Stifle joint; 21. Tibia;
22. Tarsal bones; 23. Hocks; 24. Digits; 25. Tail (coccygeal vertebrae)

is why it is possible for a dog to get very highly placed at one show
and be unplaced at the next; in fact this is what showing is all
about.

At present we do not have any specialist judges for Border
Collies, except those judging trials. To judge and award top
honours to a collie one considers to be typical of the breed will be
a rewarding experience, but should only be attempted when one is
confident that sufficient knowledge of the breed has been gained,
but to be the owner or exhibitor will be both rewarding and
thrilling.

A great responsibility rests upon the shoulders of the judges appointed to evaluate the Border Collie exhibits at the first few

shows. At present most are what are known in the show world as all-rounders. These are judges with a vast experience in many breeds, but they would be the first to admit that they are only real specialists in a few. However experienced they may be, all of them will now start from the same point, since none will have judged these dogs under the new Breed Standard. Few will ever have had any experience of the breed in its working capacity. Many of them may have judged Border Collies abroad, indeed I have myself, but they have been judged to the Breed Standard and type existing in that particular country. We now have British dogs requiring to be judged to a British Standard. The responsibilities are to see that the points in the new Standard are faithfully adhered to. I had the honour to judge the first separate Border Collie classes which were scheduled at the Ashford and Faversham Open Show at Maidstone on 7 November 1976. I was very conscious of my responsibilities in this appointment and made up my mind that whatever the consequences, if the exhibits did not come up to my interpretation of the correct type according to the Standard, I would not hesitate to withhold the awards. There were only three exhibits for me to evaluate and happily they were all of sufficient merit for an award.

I would advise any inexperienced but aspiring judges of this breed to attend a few sheepdog trials at either local or international level. Watch these dogs at work and observe their general behaviour outside the trial ring. You will then begin to appreciate fully how and why each part of the Standard fits the dog. He has been purpose-bred for many generations, so 'get your eye in' for the correct anatomical construction and the distinctive movement which is very important. Ignore type at this stage, for there is considerable variance here, although the top winners almost all conform to a certain type. It would be a pity if people whose only experience of this breed was limited to watching them perform in obedience ring or at exemption shows, should accept appointments to judge them. Should this happen then in no time the worst fears of those opposed to showing Border Collies would be realized. In saying this my only aim is to try to preserve the qualities for which this breed is famous. Type, quality and temperament cannot be written into any Standard but they are very important in the general make-up of the breed. A judge can only base his assessment on what he sees in front of him, so it is up to those owners who feel they have the correct type and the right temperament in their dogs to exhibit them at these first shows. With this in mind we now come to the part the exhibitors must play.

Each owner of a dog that enters for a show does so for a different reason, but the exhibitors of Border Collies at the first shows should have one aim in mind only; to try to establish the correct type. I feel very strongly that even those who are opposed to showing this breed but who feel that they have the correct type should allow the judges and the public to see them. If there are sufficient of the correct type for the judges to base their opinions on and make their awards, then matters will develop along the right lines. It will not be in the interests of the breed if at those first shows a ring full of pet-type Border Collies of all shapes and sizes are the only exhibits the judge has to evaluate.

In my opinion the Border Collie is second to none, which is why I want to help exhibitors to show them to the best possible advantage so that they may be admired as much in the show ring as they are on the pastoral scene. Let us presume, then, that you are an owner or breeder and have decided, or been persuaded, to show your collie. Here is the way you set about it. Select a fairly local show for your first effort, and if the breeder of your dog has persuaded you to enter then take his or her advice as to the best one at which to exhibit, the correct classes to enter and the method of transport. (This advice may of course seem a little premature here, as opportunities for showing these dogs may be limited for a little while yet.) Any Border Collie registered with the I.S.D.S. and the Kennel Club is now eligible to be shown in Pastoral or Any Variety Collie classes where scheduled, unless there are separate classes scheduled for this breed. All exhibits must be over six months of age and should be fully inoculated before being entered.

One word of caution here which may save you some disappointment later—many collie puppies are not sufficiently well-grown or ring-trained to be shown so early and it is better to wait until they are, rather than have hopes of a possible future champion or keen exhibitor dashed the first time out. An intending exhibitor would be well advised to attend some ring-craft classes before going to their first show. These are usually run in connection with obedience clubs, and their addresses can be obtained from the local town hall or police station, or from the Kennel Club. Attendance at a hall, mixing with other dogs and getting accustomed to strange noises and people is valuable experience. Where actual ring-craft classes are held separately these provide experience for dogs and owners. It is advisable to attend a few shows while your puppy is growing (without him of course) as in this way you can learn the procedures, or better still join a local canine society or club. You may ask 'How does one get to know about any shows?' Most shows are advertised in one of the specialist canine weekly papers—*Dog World* and *Our Dogs*—both of which are obtainable through newsagents. Local papers are worth watching too for show advertisements. You should then write to the show secretary for a schedule. In these days a stamp enclosed with your application is appreciated (sometimes it is requested), but not a stamped addressed envelope as the schedule may not fit into the one you send. Having received your entry form, fill it in carefully, checking all details; then post it, together with the entry fee, as early as possible before the closing date. If you have not yet received your dog's registration card from the Kennel Club, put N.A.F. (name applied for) after the name of the dog. If the breeder from whom you purchased the dog has already registered him and you are just waiting for the return of the transfer certificate from the Kennel Club, then enter the initials T.A.F. (transfer applied for) after the name of the dog. For a puppy you may need to add T.A.R.A.F. which means you have applied to have it transferred to the Active Register if you are the breeder. A word of warning here. Transfers can take many weeks, sometimes months to arrive back, but if your cheque has been passed don't panic, just proceed as above.

In due course you will receive your exhibitor's pass for the show, although some show societies have now stopped sending out passes —but this is mentioned in the schedule. If it is a benched show the number of your bench in the appropriate section is usually shown on the card. If it is an unbenched show, arrive at the hall or showground early in order to procure a seat at the ringside and a suitable place for your dog to lie down without being disturbed. It is always a wise policy to aim to get to a show at least half an hour before the advertised starting time. Your dog can be exercised to relieve himself and get used to all the strange surroundings, noises and people. Young dogs will often not relieve themselves away from home, but should an accident occur in the ring do not feel embarrassed or make the dog feel guilty. This frequently happens, so call one of the ring stewards and he will deal with it. Never leave your dog unattached on his bench until you are certain he has settled, and even then ask someone to keep an eye on him.

The feeding of a show dog differs a little from that of a working dog. The show dog is expected to carry more body or weight, which is usually referred to as show condition, as opposed to lean or hard-working condition. It is always said that one must both breed and feed correctly if one wants to own top class dogs. The breeder should be able to give you full advice on the feeding of your dog and you will be overwhelmed by ideas on this subject by other exhibitors. Listen to all these theories but do not necessarily act upon them. My own advice is to give plenty of good wholesome sensible food, but do not add extra vitamins or other additives unless specially recommended by your vet. In most cases these will either cause the unbalancing of the diet or be simply a waste of money, only passing through the dog undigested. Most of the reliable dog food manufacturers today produce well-balanced diets, stating all the ingredients and vitamins. It is a wise precaution not to feed your dog on the day of the show until you return home. If, however, it has been a long day and it will be late when you return you can give the dog a hard boiled egg or two after being judged—if he will take them. On returning home your first move should to be allow the dog a free run to relieve himself. He will then probably want a drink, because quite often a young dog will do neither while away from home. He can then have his meal.

Presuming you have fed and exercised your dog correctly and he has had a few lessons in ring behaviour he should now be ready for the final touches of grooming the coat. Unless a dog is in good health and full coat, no amount of grooming will bring up that extra lustre required in the show ring. To show a dog out of coat puts him at a disadvantage. Regular grooming each day not only gets out all the dead hairs but also stimulates and tones up the skin and muscles. Washing the white parts with plain soap and water and rinsing well afterwards is all that is required. Never use washing-up liquid or detergent on a dog—they affect the sensitive skin. Ideally a collie should be kept in show condition at all times, with just that extra 'spit and polish' being needed for the show (a rub with a piece of pure silk will add final gloss). There are a confusing number of coat preparations on the market but I have always found rainwater is the cheapest and the best. If not available I have to make do with tap water. Having first brushed the dog to remove any loose hair, dust or mud, wet the dog all over with a sponge. For a dog from an industrial area which may have some grease or soot in the coat due to atmospheric conditions, add some surgical spirit to the water. I personally never bath a dog before a show as it tends to soften the coat and make it lie too flat, but the white parts such as legs, feet and chest or mane may be washed if needed; while still wet apply chalk block, talcum powder or starch (not instant). If the dog is kept well brushed this should not be necessary, but if it is, then care must be taken not to get any on the black coat to dull it. Dry the dog with a chamois leather for preference. With a good brush groom the coat away from the lay of the hair both upwards and towards the head. The dog will then usually give himself a good shake and the hair will assume its natural position, but the whole coat will really stand out. It might be worth mentioning here that if you bring to the show a spray bottle or aerosol can of one of the many coat dressings to be applied at the last moment before going into the ring, make sure that the eyes and ears of your dog are protected from the spray fumes by being covered with a towel, but water is really all the dressing needed for a Border Collie coat. All grooming tools should be kept scrupulously clean, and dead hairs removed. Clean bedding is also essential to good health and coat condition. Other tips or aspects of grooming and preparation can only be learned by experience. In fact you will find that you learn something each time you attend a show, but beware—this 'show-bug' is very infectious!

PROCEDURE IN THE RING

The behaviour or manners of both dogs and exhibitors is under constant gaze from the ringside, so make sure that neither of you fails in this respect. With Border Collies being so new to the show ring, the eyes of the world will be on them, so make sure that both you and your dog create the right impact. Smoking in the ring, long conversations or chastisement of your dog are all considered bad manners, and for someone outside the ring to try to attract the attention of the dog inside is to break a Kennel Club rule.

When your class is announced and your number called (if this is not on your pass it will be found in the show catalogue which you can purchase at the door), enter the ring, always with your dog on your left side, and obtain your number card from the ring steward who will direct you where to stand. A number clip or safety pin is needed for displaying the card. Remember that from that moment onward your dog is on show. Allow plenty of space between yourself and the exhibitor in front of you; keep one eye on your dog and the other on the judge and have a toy or titbit in your hand or pocket to keep the dog's attention. Usually a judge will ask the whole class to move their exhibits around the ring, so follow the one in front at a reasonable distance. At other times a judge will walk down the line of exhibits to get an idea of the overall quality in that class. At this stage your dog should be showing itself and both of you should be in the position indicated (see Plate 13a). When moving, the dog should be at arm's length away from you, trotting at his own correct pace, neither pulling forward nor backward on his lead. Here is where your home training will pay dividends.

The judge then requires each exhibitor to bring the dog up to him for close examination so that he can evaluate the dog according to the points of the Breed Standard. You will then be asked to move your dog away from the judge and bring him back, or to move him in a triangle. A word of advice here. Try to position yourself either at the end of the line of exhibits or fairly far down, as this gives you time to see the other exhibitors showing their dogs, and make mental notes of what they do and what the judge requires. Some judges will ask you the age of your dog. To ascertain both ear carriage and expression, some judges prefer to attract the dog's attention themselves, others prefer the handler to do so.

When all the exhibits in the class have been seen by the judge, the steward will ask the class to 'show their dogs'. This means getting your dog's full attention and posing him where he can be seen to best advantage by both judge and spectators. Plate 13a is a good illustration of how to train a young pup for the correct positioning of dog and handler. The judge will then indicate which dogs he or she requires either for further examination if the classes are large, or to place for the final awards.

If you have not been seen by the judge or have any other reason for complaint, report at once to the ring steward. Should your dog be successful and be placed among the first three, judges' comments will appear in the report of the show in one or both of the dog papers the following week. Should he not be placed, it is quite in order for you to ask the judge's opinion of him when judging is completed. It is worth remembering that you take home the same dog as you brought whatever the comments. If the dog has lost through your inefficient grooming or handling, then set about improving both.

Useful Accessories for Showing

For all types of shows it will be found useful to keep a special 'show bag' which holds a separate set of grooming tools from those used at home, as well as the items listed below. A zip-type bag is preferable as things will not fall out, and the dog's nose will not dip in; if possible it should also be waterproof. I myself use one which has a separate pocket outside, into which I put my show schedule after I have posted the entry form, making sure I have ticked off the classes entered and the names of the dogs (when entering more than one). As soon as the show passes arrive, I pop them in here too—it is so easy to forget them on the day, or mislay the schedule, and then panic ensues as one tries to remember where the show is being held, what time it starts and so on. Here is a list of some essentials:

1. A towel for your dog and a small toilet bag for yourself.
2. A plastic container of drinking water for your dog, and a small bowl (some dogs will not drink water from another district, and like babies it sometimes upsets them at first). A package or container for the titbits (chicken or liver are favourites). A flask and some sandwiches or other refreshments for yourself. This is not necessary at club shows where the refreshments are usually home-made and the club relies on the profit from this department to help with the show expenses.
3. At a benched or unbenched show some owners provide a small rug or blanket for their dogs. Personally I prefer to use newspaper for this purpose; it is easier to carry and more hygienic. As there is no need to bring it home it lessens the risk of returning with pests or diseases picked up at the show.
4. Collar and lead will, of course, be on the dog; a choke chain type is advisable for the journey since collies are past masters at slipping backwards out of collars. A small round leather collar should also be worn, with a name and address on it in case of accidents either at the show or in transit. It will also be needed for attaching the benching chain to, as choke collars should never be used for this purpose.
5. A benching chain. These can be obtained at stalls at most of the shows. A dog can chew through a leather lead or it can easily become untied. A small ring is provided at the back of

181

the bench for attaching the chain. Make sure it is fixed on securely, neither so short that the dog cannot lie down, nor so long that he can come forward and jump off the bench with possible injury to himself.

6. A thin leather or nylon show lead for the show ring. I recommend this because to show the dog on a heavy chain or lead gives the impression that he is fierce or difficult to control.

7. Scissors (blunted ends) in case of any last minute trimming being necessary.

8. Clean brush and comb, chalk block, whitening, starch or talcum powder.

I always take a separate pair of shoes (in a plastic bag) to wear at the show, and pop them back into the bag before returning home. On arriving home I dip the dog's feet (and the show shoes) in a bowl of water with a mild disinfectant before letting the dogs out for exercise. I feel it is a precaution worth taking, especially if one has young stock at home that has not yet been fully inoculated.

A veterinary surgeon and a first aid post are catered for at most big shows so there is little need to include anything in this direction, but a small tin of plasters, some aspirins and a packet of tissues can sometimes be very useful.

The interim Breed Standard which follows here is the one now approved by the Kennel Club from a combination of several proposed standards submitted to them from various interested bodies including the recognized one from the Australian Kennel Club. It is quite possible that this Standard will need further ratification in the future, but that will be the job of a breed club to sort out with the Kennel Club. Explanations of the various points of this Standard will be found on pp. 44–56.

Amended Interim Standard for Border Collie arising from Breed Standards Sub-Committee Meeting 11 November 1980

CHARACTERISTICS—Should be neither nervous nor aggressive, but keen, alert, responsive and intelligent.

GENERAL APPEARANCE—The general appearance should be that

of a well proportioned dog, the smooth outline showing quality, gracefulness and perfect balance, combined with sufficient substance to convey the impression that it is capable of endurance. Any tendency to coarseness or weediness is undesirable.

HEAD AND SKULL—Skull fairly broad, occiput not pronounced. Cheeks should not be full or rounded. The muzzle, tapering to the nose, should be moderately short and strong, and the skull and foreface should be approximately the same length. Nose black, except in the case of a brown or chocolate coloured dog when it may be brown. Nostrils well developed. Stop very distinct.

EYES—The eyes should be set wide apart, oval shaped of moderate size and brown in colour, except in the case of merles where one or both, or part of one or both, may be blue. The expression mild, keen, alert and intelligent.

EARS—The ears should be of medium size and texture, set well apart. Carried erect or semi-erect and sensitive in their use.

MOUTH—The teeth should be strong, with perfect regular and complete scissor bite, i.e., the upper teeth closely overlapping the lower teeth and set square to the jaws.

NECK—The neck should be of good length, strong and muscular, slightly arched and broadening to the shoulders.

FOREQUARTERS—Front legs parallel when viewed from front, pasterns sloping slightly when viewed from side. Bone should be strong but not heavy. Shoulders well laid back, elbows close to the body.

BODY—Athletic in appearance, ribs well sprung, chest deep and rather broad, loins deep, muscular, but not tucked up. Body slightly longer than height at shoulder.

HINDQUARTERS—The hindquarters should be broad and muscular, in profile sloping gracefully to the set on of the tail. The thighs should be long, deep and muscular with well turned stifles and strong hocks, well let down. From hock to ground the hind legs should be well boned and parallel when viewed from the rear.

FEET—Oval in shape, pads deep, strong and sound, toes arched and close together. Nails short and strong.

GAIT—Movement free, smooth and tireless, with a minimum lift of feet, conveying the impression of the ability to move with great stealth and speed.

TAIL—The tail should be moderately long, the bone reaching at least to the hock joint, set on low, well furnished and with an upward swirl towards the end, completing the graceful contour and balance of the dog. The tail may be raised in excitement but never carried over the back.

COAT—There are two varieties of coat, one moderately long, the other smooth. In both, the topcoat should be dense and medium textured, the undercoat short, soft and dense giving good weather resistance. In the moderately long coated variety, abundant coat forms a mane, breeching and brush. On face, ears, forelegs (except for feather) hindlegs from hock to ground, the hair should be short and smooth.

COLOUR—A variety of colours is permissible, but white should never predominate.

SIZE—Ideal height: Dogs 53 cm (21 in). Bitches slightly less.

FAULTS—Any departure from the foregoing points should be considered a fault and the seriousness with which the fault be regarded should be in exact proportion to its degree.

NOTE—*Male animals should have two apparently normal testicles fully descended into the scrotum.*

New Working Test for Show Border Collies (1982)

In an effort to preserve the working instincts and abilities of this breed the I.S.D.S., the Border Collie Club of G.B. and the Southern Border Collie Club requested the K.C. to introduce a herding test whereby Show Ch. Border collies can qualify for the title of Full Ch. This was agreed upon in April 1982, with the provision that it be reviewed after one year.

CONDITIONS—The test will be limited to dogs who have qualified for entry in the K.C. Stud Book by gaining a First, Second or Third place in Limit or Open classes at Ch. Shows where Challenge certificates are on offer. The layout of the course and the provision of the two judges for this test to be the responsibility of the I.S.D.S.

TEST EXERCISES—1. Outrun—max. distance 200 yds.   20 points
                 2. Lift (5 sheep)   10
                 3. A straight fetch past a post to the
                    handler   20
                 4. Drive (max. 100 yds)   30
                 5. A gated pen (12′ × 6′)   20
                                        ———

Time allowed 15 minutes. Pass mark required 60.   100
                                                               ———

EXEMPTIONS—Dogs/Bitches which have gained titles in the show ring but have been placed 1st–7th at an Open Sheep Dog Trial affiliated to the I.S.D.S. or those who have qualified for the National or International Sheep Dog Trials after 1982, are exempt from this K.C. test.

Should it be requested provision can be made for testing the herding ability of these dogs on other livestock.

The first Challenge Certificates on offer for Border Collies was at Crufts 1982 judged by Mrs C. Sutton in place of the appointed judge Mr Harry Glover, who was too ill to officiate. The winner of the Dog Challenge Certificate was Mr Cosme and Mrs Collis's Tilehouse Cassius of Beagold and the Bitch Certificate went to Mr Eric Broadhurst's Tracelyn Gal.

The first Champion Border Collies were crowned on the same day by Mr A. Finlay, a well known personality in shepherding circles, at the National Working Breeds Show on July 17th. The honours went once again to Tilehouse Cassius of Beagold, but the first Bitch Champion was Mrs Simpson's Muirend Border Dream. It is interesting to note that both collies are from good working stock and I feel as proud as Mrs Simpson to have bred the first Border Collie Show Champion.

Chapter 6

BORDER COLLIES OUTSIDE THE UNITED KINGDOM

Each year I receive numerous letters from abroad, some passed on to me by other people or societies, requesting information on the origin of some local overseas shepherding breed, and almost all say they believe the breed in question is of Scottish descent. Regrettably I can rarely help them with much more information on the breed than I have laid before you in this book. I sincerely hope that any overseas breeders or handlers of Border Collies who happen to read it will find it helpful for their researches.

It will be understood that there were local dogs used for herding sheep and cattle in every part of the world long before Britons or the Border Collie arrived on the scene. When we had a great British Empire it was only natural that our great shepherding traditions should play a part in it, and sheepfarmers from these islands with their dogs, settled in many lands and made their influence felt. The Empire faded, but the superiority of our sheep-dogs strengthened.

Originally many of the dogs brought out by these settlers were from the same rather mixed bag as they were in this country, so it is no wonder that people trying to establish origins run into difficulties. However, as time progressed the superior working ability of the new strain of sheepdog that we now accept as the Border Collie was being recognized in places like Canada, New Zealand and Australia, and some good dogs and bitches were exported to these countries where they not only adapted quickly to local conditions but made excellent foundation stock. The only way to success is to breed from this type of stock, so the present-day overseas buyers are able to start on the right lines. Those who sell their valued dogs must have great heart-searchings first, but it is very rewarding to see the progeny of these exports doing so well in other parts of the world. When visiting or competing over-seas it must sometimes cause British sheepfarmers to reflect that it may have taken them three or four generations of breeding, culling and selection to make a champion, yet here, possibly from their own stock, their rivals sometimes have a champion in the first generation. The confidence placed in our British stock and the knowledge that only the best has been exported compensates for any remorse.

One question that keeps cropping up concerns the origin of the Kelpie. Many people regard them as having originated from a cross between a collie and a dingo. The more I research into this problem the more convinced I become that the Kelpie probably existed even before the collie. His type was certainly known in North Africa thousands of years ago, but we do not know by what name. They were a lightly built type of shepherd dog, red or fox-coloured. There is some evidence that they were brought back to Scotland during the Napoleonic wars and intermingled with local dogs. The resulting progeny were named 'Kelpie'—a Gaelic word for a spirited animal like a colt or a heifer. If one considers that the country folk who spoke Gaelic were known to call the farm dogs 'collies' it is not difficult to imagine that they would call this new type of farm or sheepdog a 'kelpie', just making that slight word variation, as he was known to be a lighter-built dog. Many were exported to Australia, but I can find no evidence that they were of Australian origin.

Further evidence to support this theory was supplied by my great-uncle James Bourchier, whom I mentioned earlier. He believed that a few Pariah or shepherd dogs of the countries on the south-east shores of the Mediterranean were actually imported into Scotland and when crossed with the local collies some of the resulting litters produced smooth brown or brindle-coloured puppies. He maintained that these were the original smooth collies and that the local people gave them the name of Kelpies. Smooth-coated varieties were almost unknown among Highland Collies before this time, only among the Lowland or drover's dogs. This theory was explained to me by my mother who had kept many of the letters Uncle James sent home. As with so many other matters regarding the origin of collies, this is only speculation, but it does have a strong claim to credibility. These dogs are often referred to as Pie dogs in much the same way as our own pastoral dogs were called curs, but in fact most of these nomadic herdsmen kept and bred a very pure strain of Pariah dog. Furthermore, as we know the collie genes always appear to be dominant in the progeny of any collie cross it is therefore a strong possibility that this was the case.

This theory may also give some credibility to the report that Kelpies were then exported to Australia. Perhaps the exporters or importers felt that they were more suited to the climatic conditions. In 1800 a man named Hall imported a pair of smooth-coated blue merle collies. These were mated to the imported Kelpies and the resulting progeny were known as Hall's Heelers and held by many to be the original parents of the Australian cattle dogs. To judge by the appearance of these dogs today I would have thought this was a strong possibility. I often see it suggested that Kelpies originated from collies exported to Australia, which were then crossed with dingos. I have been informed by reliable authorities that if such a mating did take place no litter would result, as is also so in the case of a dog and a fox cross. A domestic animal differs from the wild animal in genotype and inheritance factors, which gives even more support to the theory regarding Hall's heelers and the cattle dogs.

Just a few years ago my husband and I visited relatives in Western Australia. We found it almost impossible to take in the vastness of that great country, for some of the farms or stations cover areas as large as the United Kingdom. On one of our tours to the high rainfall region of Esperance we paid a brief visit to a station covering 16,000 acres; it carried about 400 head of cattle and I cannot remember how many thousands of sheep. We were told that the neighbouring station covered 500,000 acres and carried 15,000 Merino sheep. Flocks or herds of this size need different management from ours in this country. The flockmasters are mounted on good fast local ponies or travel in open trucks. At mustering times the bosses often use light aircraft for spotting stray animals in the crags or gullies, and then the dog is sent to collect them. The dogs that accompany the stock may travel anything up to 100 miles in a day and possibly more. Collies in the United Kingdom often cover this distance too, but not in the same climatic conditions.

Depending on the type of stock or location these dogs are often Kelpies or the Australian cattle dogs, but the Border Collies usually outnumber these. The dogs are trained for special tasks with the stock at the stations or on the drives; there are heading dogs, leading, huntaway and backing dogs, to say nothing of the handy and trial dogs. Many of these tasks were new to me but I would not care to attempt to describe them here without sufficient knowledge of the purpose of each.

Our guide on one of these tours thought he would tell us a doggy story to compensate for his lack of knowledge on the subject. He told us: 'An aborigine once owned a collie reputed to be over thirty years old, with corns on its arse from sitting around, it was only capable of moving from one patch of shade to another. Someone wanted to shoot it, but the womenfolk prevented it.' Well, it served me right for asking about the dogs!

The show Border Collies that I judged and came into contact with in Australia were of a different type to those I saw working and differed considerably from our own types over here, being stockier and shorter on the hocks; they also appeared to carry more coat and were certainly well groomed and turned out.

New Zealand sheep farmers make a great study of their collies in the rôle of sheepdogs, and like Australians they breed types specially suited to perform various tasks connected with flock management and the difficult terrain. Dogs and bitches exported by some of our leading handlers give good accounts of themselves at trials too.

Canada, the United States of America and parts of South America all have Border Collies—either recently imported or established strains whose pedigrees can be traced back to our own Hemp. There are many interesting books about the breed and the local methods of working, written by people from all the above countries, and in his delightful little book on sheepdogs the well-known Irish handler Lionel Pennefather has given us a great deal of information on Border Collies in South Africa. Regrettably my own experience of the collies in these countries is limited to brief visits to a few farms, because of the inevitable travel restrictions imposed by the great distances which have to be covered.

Let us move from lands where the grazing ratio in some areas is one sheep per 1,000 acres to the West Indies where the ratio is more likely to be a few feet per sheep and where most are tethered. Under these conditions the useful black-bellied sheep of these islands have no need of a dog to control them, yet there are many Border Collies kept as pets and being worked in obedience tests. The owners are extremely proud of their dogs and their bloom and condition are magnificent.

The Falkland Islands boast as many folk and dogs descended from Scottish shepherding families as almost anywhere else in the world, but the climate and grazing conditions are very different.

Air travel has helped to stimulate interest, making it a little easier for our handlers to compete in trials overseas, but the cost of such a venture gets daily more expensive. We should be most grateful to those who have already taken up this challenge and kept the flag of the British collie as a superior sheepdog flying to good account. To fully appreciate the planning and cost involved in such an undertaking we must realize the work involved too. To begin with, the handler and his dog will be away from duty on his own farm. Then the health arrangements for himself and his dog must be completed, flights booked, kennelling arrangements made both on the plane and on landing, and hundreds of other details completed. Finally there is the sad parting from the dog when he has to go into quarantine on arriving home. I feel sure that many dogs must feel totally confused at this new and restricted way of life, cut off from work, when they are in the peak of condition.

On the continent of Europe the Border Collie is becoming a big challenge to many local shepherding dogs because of its smart working ability and strong resistance to diseases. This also makes him a popular pet. In Holland a Border Collie Club has recently been formed and I know of others about to be set up in other Western European countries. Since recognition the popularity of the Border Collie overseas has risen rapidly and I get inquiries almost daily for information on the breed. Perhaps one day I will be able to make a detailed study of Border Collies outside the United Kingdom.

Index

Agriculture, Ministry of, 89
Alderson, Lance, 104
Alexandra Palace, 98
Allen, C. T., 103
Alsatian (German Shepherd), 78–9, 84, 86
anal glands, 128
artificial insemination, 150–1
Ashford and Faversham Open Show, 1976, 174
Ashton, Ellis, 97–8
Australia, 73–4, 110, 186–7, 188–9
Australian cattle dogs, 188, 189

Bala, 94, 95, 98–9, 108
ban dogs, 31
Barnett, Dr Keith, 128, 129
BBC, 104
Bearded Collie, 34, 54, 72
Bective, Countess of, 40
bedding, 136
Bedford, Dukes of, 35
benched shows, 171
Best, Captain, 95–6
Birmingham Show, 1860, 170
blindness, 55, 128–30
body, Breed Standard, 50, 184
Border Collie Club, 19, 21, 43
Bourchier, James, 15–16, 33, 187–8
Breed Standard, 42–56, 174–5, 182–5
breeding, legal requirements, 61–63; registration, 56–61; regis-
tered prefixes, 57–8; sheepdog gundog crosses, 38–9; choice of breeding stock, 116–20; stud dogs, 145–7, 148–51; mating, 142–7; pregnancy, 147, 151–3; whelping, 156–61
Byrness, 95

Canada, 186–7, 190
canine distemper, 123–4
canine hepatitis, 124
canker, 132
Cardigan Corgi, 19, 34
Carnwath, 95
castration, 120
Catherine Plantagenet, 24
Challenge Certificates, 172–3
championship shows, 171
coat, 148–9; Breed Standard, 54–55, 184; grooming, 131, 132–3, 134, 178–9
Cocker Spaniel, 17–18
collars, 82
collie, etymology, 26–7
Collie Eye Anomaly (C.E.A.), 55, 128
'collie gatherings', 92
collie nose, 127
colour, Breed Standard, 53–4, 184; inheritance, 149
corgis, 18–19, 34
Cornwall, 34
Cotswolds, 33

192